LORDS OF CREATION

THE GOLDEN AMAZON SAGA

1. *World Beneath Ice*
2. *Lord of Atlantis*
3. *Triangle of Power*
4. *The Amethyst City*
5. *Daughter of the Amazon*
6. *Quorne Returns*
7. *The Central Intelligence*
8. *The Cosmic Crusaders*
9. *Parasite Planet*
10. *World Out of Step*
11. *The Shadow People*
12. *Kingpin Planet*
13. *World in Reverse*
14. *Dwellers in Darkness*
15. *World in Duplicate*
16. *Lords of Creation*
17. *Duel with Colossus*
18. *Standstill Planet*
19. *Ghost World*
20. *Earth Divided*
21. *Chameleon Planet* (with Philip Harbottle)

LORDS OF CREATION

THE GOLDEN AMAZON SAGA, BOOK SIXTEEN

JOHN RUSSELL FEARN

Edited by Philip Harbottle

THE BORGO PRESS

MMXIV

LORDS OF CREATION

FIRST BORGO PRESS EDITION

Published by Wildside Press LLC

www.wildsidebooks.com

CONTENTS

THE GOLDEN AMAZON 7

PREFACE, by Philip Harbottle. 19

CHAPTER 1: COSMIC TRAP 26

CHAPTER 2: THE RED PLANET 47

CHAPTER 3: ESCAPE INTO SPACE. 68

CHAPTER 4: PLANET OF MONSTROSITIES 88

CHAPTER 5: BODY SWAP. 111

CHAPTER 6: THE SURVIVOR. 132

CHAPTER 7: ALL-IN-ONE. 155

CHAPTER 8: MENTAL COMPULSION 177

ABOUT THE AUTHOR. 213

THE GOLDEN AMAZON

by Philip Harbottle

In 1943 British writer John Russell Fearn decided to quit writing for the American pulp science fiction magazines, and to concentrate instead on books for the English market. Within a very few years he became established as a leading novelist in several genres, not only science fiction, but also mystery and detective fiction, and westerns.

His first new SF novel, *The Golden Amazon*, was published by World's Work in April 1944. In this story, a little girl of three years of age is made the subject of an idealistic scientist's illegal glandular experiments. The scientist's dream is to end world wars by creating a woman devoid of the usual lusts and frailties of mankind, who upon reaching maturity would institute a benign scientific rule. But the apparently successful experiment has a flaw: it instills into the girl a hatred for all men, and a ruthless cruelty. Her supernatural scientific gifts enable her to master atomic power, and practically leads her to destroy the world. She breaks the will and strength of men, and elevates women to positions of wealth and power. She also discovers human synthesis, and by this means she is able to escape retribution when she is eventually overthrown. She is seen to collapse and die, a victim of consuming ketabolism, echoing the memorable finale of Rider Haggard's *She*. In actuality, it was only her synthetic image, and this paved the way for the *Golden Amazon Returns*, and further sequels.

Fearn sold reprint rights in the first novel to the prestigious Canadian magazine, the Toronto *Star Weekly*. The magazine carried a special Comics Supplement, the centre section of which was a 'complete novel', published in newspaper format. Aimed at a general readership, the novels were written by the top popular novelists of the day, including John Dickson Carr, Ellery Queen, and P. G. Wodehouse. They sold hundreds of thousands of copies, and the novels were syndicated to several American newspapers in the Maine and New York areas. The Amazon novels enjoyed extraordinary popularity (especially with Canadian housewives), and ran for the next sixteen years following the appearance of the first novel in the March 3, 1945 issue, ending with Fearn's sudden death in September 1960, aged only fifty-two. His final two Amazon novels appeared posthumously.

During Fearn's lifetime, only the first six novels were published in British hardcover editions from the World's Work in England, after appearing in the *Star Weekly*. This was because the publishers discontinued their entire fiction line in 1954. However, the Amazon novels continued to appear in the *Star Weekly*, eventually notching up twenty-four titles.

Fearn had resold paperback rights to the Canadian publisher Harlequin Books, but after publishing only the first three titles, they stopped publishing SF and other genre fiction to concentrate on their famous Romances line.

Meanwhile, as early as 1949, Fearn had realized that the Amazon series had the potential to run indefinitely. This presented him with a problem, however. The 'origin story' of the Golden Amazon was conceived and actually set during the Second World War. Subsequent novels were written during the war and the immediate postwar period, and projected their stories only a few decades into the future.

He very astutely realized that to keep ahead of reality, he needed to move the Amazon *further* into the future—first into the outer solar system, and thence to the stars. So with the seventh novel, he introduced a new main character, Abna of Atlantis—someone equally intelligent, and even stronger than herself. These dynamics provided him with an *interstellar* canvas, thus ensuring that the series would remain ahead of reality.

Fearn's strategy was a great success, and the Amazon novels retained their popularity, ending only with his tragically early death in 1960. By then he had written a further twenty Amazon novels and made preliminary notes for his next (which would later be written by Fearn's biographer, Philip Harbottle).

Long after Fearn's death, his entire Amazon series would eventually see print from the pioneering US small press Gryphon Books in limited paperback editions, and later by the Canadian Battered Silicon Dispatch Box small press in their hardcover Omnibus series.

This new Borgo Press paperback series will be the first trade edition of all twenty-one of these later novels by Fearn, beginning with the seventh novel in the original series. First published in 1949 as *Conquest of the Amazon*, I have edited it slightly as *World Beneath Ice* (The Golden Amazon Saga, Book One) so that it can be read and enjoyed by new readers who may be totally unfamiliar with what had gone before. Subsequent novels have also been slightly edited for modern readers.

The publishers hope that this new series may create many more "fans of the Amazon." Meanwhile, any reader interested in seeking out the earlier six Golden Amazon novels will find that they are readily available on the internet, and in numerous earlier paperback and hardcover editions.

* * * *

To date, readers can enjoy the following new Borgo Press editions:

Book One: *World Beneath Ice*

In destroying the threat of an alien invasion, the

Golden Amazon had inadvertently caused a decline in the sun's heat, encasing Earth in an ice sheet that threatens to eliminate humanity. The Amazon encounters Abna, a descendant of Atlantis, stronger and even more scientifically advanced than she, and the ruler of an Atlantean colony still surviving in a protected environment on Jupiter. She refuses his offer of marriage, but agrees to form an alliance in order to restore the sun and save the Earth. One thing that Abna has not told the Amazon is that all the females of his race have been wiped out by a bacilli infection....

Book Two: *Lord of Atlantis*

A gigantic ridge of land rises from the Atlantic floor, causing massive tidal waves on either side of the ocean. Even stranger, both England and America are then assailed by an invasion of prehistoric monsters! A gigantic domed city rests on the newly risen plateau, whilst out in space an alien spacecraft orbits the Earth. Such are the mysteries and challenges facing the Golden Amazon, self-appointed governess of Earth, as she struggles to unravel the maze of mystery that was the deadly legacy of Atlantis!

Book Three: *Triangle of Power*

The marriage of Violet Ray Brant—better known as The Golden Amazon—and Abna of Atlantis should have ushered in an era of peace and scientific prosperity to the people of Earth. But an unexpected turn of events finds Abna betrayed and marooned on a satellite of Jupiter, and the Amazon flung far beyond the Solar System. With Earth's two protectors removed, the planet is now at the mercy of another Atlantean, the master scientist Sefner Quorne....

Book Four: *The Amethyst City*

The metaphysical union of the Amazon and Abna results in the mental creation of a fully mature daughter—Viona. Quorne, still struggling for domination, forces Viona into a marriage ceremony, and impregnates her. But with the intervention of Tarnec Brodix, a super-mind from an external universe, Quorne and Viona are separately flung into an ultra-dimensional limbo. Abna chooses to follow after his daughter, leaving the Amazon to brood over the disaster, alone in the Amethyst City of Saturn.

Book Five: *Daughter of the Amazon*

A miscalculation by the super-mathematician Tarnec Brodix destroys his universe, and the fault spreads into the Earth universe in the form of a Dark Tide of Absolute Nothingness. Unable to save himself, Brodix transfers his knowledge into the one mind powerful enough to receive it: that if Sefian, the son who has been born to Viona and Quorne. Sefian rapidly evolves, and, no longer human, after saving the Earth universe, vanishes into the greater universe, to seek new challenges. Then the Amazon is confronted with a further puzzle—a large section of the planet Neptune is discovered to be an exact duplicate of the Earth!

Book Six: *Quorne Returns*

The bacterial intelligences of Neptune plan to conquer Earth by replacing humans in key positions with alien duplicates. The Neptunians are themselves subjugated by the sinister Atlantean scientist, Sefner Quorne. Alerted to the threat, the Golden Amazon hits back by creating the ultimate doomsday weapon—only to precipitate a reprisal from the denizens of another universe....

Book Seven: *The Central Intelligence*

The Golden Amazon's arch-enemy, Sefner Quorne, discovers that all mental gifts, such as memory and creativity, are something that is broadcast throughout the universe by a Central Intelligence—and then interpreted according to the quality of the individual brain of the recipient. At the surprising suggestion of his wife, Viona, the Amazon's daughter, Quorne travels with her to the very center of the universe, in order to wrest the secrets of mentality from the very source itself!

Book Eight: *The Cosmic Crusaders*

The Golden Amazon renounces all ties with Earth when, together with her husband, Abna, and her daughter, Viona, she sets off on a journey to explore the cosmos. On the strange worlds of Alpha Centauri, she encounters Mizanu, the embodiment of evil—a planet-sized hypertrophied brain! Its baleful, crushing mental power threatens to reach out beyond the double-system of Alpha and Proxima Centauri to engulf the Earth and all the other inhabited planets of the galaxy—unless the Amazon can destroy it first!

Book Nine: *Parasite Planet*

The Cosmic Crusaders discover a fantastic world of mental parasites drawing form and substance from our own Earth, fifty light years distant. The planet is ruled by a being identical to the Golden Amazon herself—but an Amazon who's coldly scientific and vicious, mirroring the original Amazon as she had once been early in her career. Inevitably, they become locked in a deadly duel—to the death!

Book Ten: *World Out of Step*

The Cosmic Crusaders find themselves on a planet that seems mysteriously not to conform with natural law, a world out of step with the universe. It leaps ahead into time at unexpected moments, thereby suddenly adding many years of age to the flower-like inhabitants, and killing tens of thousands of individuals through death and old age. In trying to find the alien menace responsible, The Golden Amazon and her fellow Crusaders are flung backwards and forwards through time and space, threatening their own survival....

Book Eleven: *The Shadow People*

The Cosmic Crusaders discover a planet whose people are subject to a baleful influence from outer space that sweeps across their world—and for a brief while embraces every man, woman and child. It stirs the emotions of the sexes against each other. Men desire only to destroy women, and women men. Only those with higher types of mind are able to build a resistance against it. The struggle is dire and dreadful, and leaves its victims physical and mental wrecks. The less fortunate are left dead after the Wave has passed.

But when the Crusaders identify and destroy the source of the problem, they precipitate an even greater menace....

Book Twelve: *Kingpin Planet*

The Cosmic Crusaders are plunged into a strange new space, where all the probabilities of electronic law were strangely altered, a complete and stunning inversion of the so-called natural laws. They discover the mysterious silver planet of Tuca, and deep below its surface they find an enigmatic machine—the legacy of a vanished race. Masters of science, they had overreached themselves by constructing a strange machine that could alter the very laws of nature and electronic probability. The machine had ultimately destroyed them, and blasted a neighboring planet into a cosmic cinder—and unless the Cosmic Crusaders can stop it, it may well destroy the entire universe!

Book Thirteen: *World in Reverse*

Continuing their cosmic crusade amongst the stars, the Golden Amazon and her companions discover a planet in another space where living beings are being synthetically created. The mystery deepens with the discovery that the synthetic race is evolving backwards! Determined to solve these mysteries, the Crusaders find themselves up against the Mithons, a sadistic alien race led by a being known as the Supreme One. Can the Amazon save the day?

Book Fourteen: *Dwellers in Darkness*

Voyaging into a sector of interstellar space plunged into total darkness, the Cosmic Crusaders encounter a powerful and sinister mastermind, who is regarded as a God by the race he has forced to evolve without eyes. And not content with shaping the evolution of their bodies, the mastermind has also impressed on their minds an urge to conquer and dominate...

Book Fifteen: *World in Duplicate*

In the depths of the Milky Way, the Cosmic Crusaders discover yet another mysterious planet—this time a world that appears to be a duplicate of Earth, birthplace of the Golden Amazon! Their investigations uncover a sinister plot by an alien race that threaten the Amazon's home world with complete annihilation!

PREFACE

by Philip Harbottle

Lords of Creation marks a true milestone in the Golden Amazon Saga. It was first published by Gary Lovisi's Gryphon Books, a New York small press, in 2004. At that time it was a paperback original, never before published—a 'lost' manuscript, of which I had the only copy in existence—Fearn's own typescript, written in 1959.

It had been found and passed to me after the death in 1982 of his widow, Carrie Fearn, whom I had represented since 1970.

My first meeting with Mrs. Fearn came about when, as editor of the British SF magazine *Vision of Tomorrow*, I was sent some hitherto unpublished and unknown Fearn short story mss by one my main contributors, Walter Gillings.

Walter himself was an ex-editor of Britain's pioneering SF magazines *Tales of Wonder* (1937-42) and *Fantasy* (1946-7). Gillings had rediscovered a number of mss accepted for those magazines, but which had remained unpublished when wartime and post-war conditions had caused their cancellation. This cache of mss had included two novelettes by Fearn, one for each magazine.

Knowing of my high regard for the author, Gillings passed the mss on to me. I immediately contacted Fearn's widow for permission to purchase and print the stories in *Vision of Tomorrow*. Mrs. Fearn invited my wife Maureen and I to visit her at the Blackpool home she had shared with her late husband, in order to complete the transaction personally. A firm friendship ensued, and it was to be the first of many visits.

Anxious to help her further financially, I implored her to search amongst Fearn's papers to see if he had left any other unpublished SF mss, which I would arrange to purchase and/or agent, on my next visit. When I called again, it was to find Mrs. Fearn visibly distressed. She confided to me her dread of entering Fearn's writing study because of the poignant memories it evoked. I learned that she had not been able to bring herself to re-enter the study for ten years, after she herself had discovered Fearn's final Amazon mss for the *Star Weekly* still in his typewriter. Not wanting to disappoint me, she had steeled herself to make a special effort. She handed me a small cache of unpublished mss, insisting "that was all there was." Naturally I respected her feelings, and thereafter the subject of the study and any other mss it might have contained was never mentioned between us. Not that I had any reason to suspect that it still contained any further mss other than those Mrs. Fearn had given me—two detective novels, a western, an incomplete SF novel, a single unpublished Golden Amazon novel, *Duel With Colossus*, together with a long SF novelette, "The Slitherers." This latter story and the two Gillings novelettes were promptly purchased, and duly appeared in *Vision of Tomorrow* in 1970—"Into the Unknown" (# 7), "Rule of the Brains" (# 10) and "The Slitherers" (# 12).

Into The Unknown was recently published by Borgo Books as one half of a Fearn SF Double volume, and *Rule of the Brains* was the title story of a new Borgo Fearn collection.

However, *Lords of Creation* was *not* amongst the mss Mrs. Fearn gave me, and I was not to learn of its existence for another dozen years!

In the years that followed, Mrs. Fearn became a dear family friend, and when our daughter Claire was born in 1972, we made frequent holiday visits over the next ten years. Childless herself, she was delighted to become Claire's honourable "Auntie." It was my pleasure and privilege as Mrs. Fearn's agent to arrange for the reprinting of many of Fearn's stories and novels, many of them in European translations—principally Italian. For those interested, full details of this period and events are set out in my recent non-fiction book, *Vultures of the Void: The Legacy.*

It was not until after Mrs. Fearn died that I learned that following Claire's birth in 1972, she had added a special codicil to her will, bequeathing all Fearn's copyrights to me after her death. I immediately requested permission from the executor to have access to Fearn's study, in order to salvage any books and papers it might contain. *I was only just in time*: the house's contents had been already been scheduled for clearance on the very morning I had telephoned!

Travelling to the Fearn home the next day, I was led into the study by the executor, Harry Masterman, whose wife had been a former lodger with Mrs. Fearn, and to whom she had left her home and personal effects. I found the room to be a veritable Aladdin's Cave of mss, books and cans of cinema films written and produced by Fearn himself, using amateur actors and actress friends. Many exciting literary discoveries were made—including two further SF novels. One of them was an earlier, novel-length version of *The Slitherers*—which I first published myself in a chap-book edition before it was later reprinted in the US by Gryphon Books, and by Ulverscroft in the UK. All of Fearn's other unpublished stories and novels— including SF, westerns, and detective fiction, have all since been reprinted or are scheduled to appear on both sides of the Atlantic. Many of the best of them have been published by Borgo Books, most notably the detective novels *The Empty Coffins, The Man Who Was Not, Reflected Glory* and *Pattern of Murder.*

This newly rediscovered material included another Amazon novel, *Lords of Creation,* but publication of this had to wait more than 20 years, until the previous 21 Amazon novels that preceded it had appeared, since they form a continuous narrative.

Lords of Creation is the first title in this Borgo series to be published *in its full, uncut length of 45,000 words*. Fearn submitted all his mss to the Toronto *Star Weekly* at 45,000 words in length, because he was hoping for later book publication, and the *Star* were happy to condense them to 40,000 words, dropping in 1956 to around 32,000 words. Unfortunately, when Fearn submitted *this* novel, in 1959, he was unaware that the *Star* were about to reduce the length of their novels still further, to just 25,000 words. I suspect that the editor adjudged that this complex novel would be too difficult to cut to almost half its length, and so it was rejected.

Fearn had resolved to try something entirely new in *Lords of Creation*. Instead of the Crusaders encountering yet another humanoid alien race, he decided to create an entirely *alien* race, completely non-human, and he further complicated his story by having the Amazon and her fellow Crusaders also undergo a complete change-over from their usual superhuman personas! Another departure was that the story was not based—either directly, or even indirectly—on any of Fearn's previously published stories. However, the story *was* based on an earlier work—but not by Fearn! Astute readers will recognize that Fearn has based his story on Frank Baum's *The Wizard of Oz*! Yes, elements from Frank Baum's famous fantasy have been reworked into an epic Fearn SF adventure novel! To find out how, you will have to read the novel for yourself.

Fortunately for posterity, when the story was rejected, the author was not informed of the pending reduction in word length, but simply that it had been adjudged unsuitable. Whereupon Fearn promptly wrote a new Amazon novel, *Duel With Colossus*, also to 45,000 words—which he quickly followed with *another* 45,000 worder, *Standstill Planet*. Evidently, after the setback, Fearn reckoned that by sending two novels he would be doubling his chance of acceptance.

His precaution was well founded, because *Duel With Colossus* was also rejected as too difficult to cut, and the mss was returned to Fearn. This was one of the mss Mrs. Fearn had found for me in 1970. However, *Standstill Planet* was readily accepted, and quickly rushed into print in March, 1960. Usually the *Star Weekly* published at least two Amazon novels a year, one in the summer and another around Christmas, but owing to the hiatus, only one novel had appeared in May 1959, much to the chagrin of their readership, who would have been expecting a second novel before the end of 1959.

When printed, *Standstill Planet* was cut to only 25,000 words. Surprisingly, it still read well—the reason being that, as printed, it was only lightly abridged. The large reduction in wordage had been mainly achieved by missing out an entire sub-plot of the novel! However, the good news for fans of the Amazon is that amongst Fearn's salvaged papers was a carbon copy of his *original full-length mss*, and *this* is the version I later restored to print.

So new fans of the Amazon can look forward to reading no less than *three* full-length 45,000 words Golden Amazon novels in the near future. They are not to be missed!

CHAPTER 1

COSMIC TRAP

The Milky Way, the First Galaxy from which Earth itself was born, was to the four travelers in the spaceship *Ultra* a blazing, incredible region of countless multi-trillions of stars and planets. From Earth, merely a hazy band spanning the night sky—but, from their nearer viewpoint, a wonder to be never forgotten. And the genius of human beings, and one human being in particular, had made possible the vast machine that could travel faster than light itself in its exploration of the interplanetary depths.

The four travelers—the self-styled Cosmic Crusaders—were inconceivably far from Earth, and not in the least concerned about the fact. They had made space their home, and their mental and physical powers—both immense beyond the normal—were dedicated to the task of helping planetary populations who found difficulty in evolving normally, either because of outside malignant agency, or purely natural causes... Even at this moment the *Ultra* was speeding away from a world that had been adversely dominated—and freed—and then destroyed. The world of Kolb. And yet, where Kolb had been, there was something peculiar, a diamond in infinity.

A diamond traced out by four points. The top and bottom points were emerald and ruby red respectively, and the left and right points were sapphire blue and golden yellow. They could have been planets, they could have been a left-over enigma from destroyed Kolb. They could have been anything... And yet— If planets, why were they set so exactly, dead opposite each other? Something mathematical seemed to be somehow responsible... And in the middle of the theoretical diamond there was nothing but the velvet blackness of infinity itself.

Time and again, as the *Ultra* hurtled onwards towards the 'diamond' the four travelers viewed and carefully examined the phenomenon through instruments without arriving at any definite conclusion.

"Any suggestions, Vi?" asked the blond-headed Abna, the tallest member of the party.

The woman at the telescope, a lithe, superbly modeled woman of apparently twenty-five, shook her head. Violet Ray Brant—otherwise the Golden Amazon—was for once in her life really puzzled, and for a woman of her incredible scientific ingenuity and imagination that was indeed something.

"No—no suggestions." She got to her feet slowly from the telescopic chair and stood thinking, her goddess-like figure in the black tights outlined against the huge observation window. "I'd say the four points are planets, yet they don't respond to the normal tests we make for planets. As for their distance away from us, I'm completely beaten. Originally I guessed a billion miles or so: now I don't think they're above a few million miles off."

"Which puts them well outside the area where Kolb originally was?" Abna asked, his enormous seven-foot figure moving over to her.

"I don't think they have any connection with Kolb. I think they're something different..." The Amazon smiled a little, a gleam of interest kindling in her violet eyes. "Different, and therefore intriguing."

Abna grinned as he looked through the window. "When the time comes that my wife says there isn't something interesting any more we'll pack up and retire," he commented. "I truly think sometimes, Vi, that you'd find interest in even a speck of dust!"

"Mmm—possible," she admitted. "That very speck of dust might be a universe on its own, full of intriguing things. And there we'd be—off again."

They were silent for a moment, both gazing onto the depths of space outside the window. Stars and cosmic dust were everywhere—and athwart it all that fantastic diamond with its four varicolored points of light... The blonde, yellow-skinned Amazon sighed gently to herself, and it was a sigh that had something of the quality of regret.

"Worried?" Abna asked, putting a great arm about her shoulders.

"Not worried exactly—just, well annoyed. I don't

like puzzles, especially scientific ones! Everything has to have an answer, but here there doesn't seem to be one. If they are not planets, what are they?"

Abna did not get the chance to answer. There was a sound in the corridor leading to the sleeping quarters and after a moment or two the copper-headed Viona, daughter of the Amazon and Abna, entered, followed by her husband Mexone. They looked at the solemn two by the window and then exchanged glances.

"I have the feeling," Viona said, with an impish smile, "that the two great minds of the Cosmic Crusaders are up against it. Your expressions say that much."

"Correct," Abna agreed calmly. "And has our bright young Viona any suggestions for getting round the problem?"

Viona chuckled. "I might have, if I knew what the problem is."

"You know quite well," the Amazon said curtly. "You and Mexone both went to bed while your father and I tried to solve the mystery of that diamond-thing ahead of us. Now the pair of you have awakened and the diamond's still there... Pretty obvious what the problem is, isn't it?"

Viona moved towards the window with Mexone beside her. For a while they contemplated the diamond shape as the *Ultra* swept on soundlessly through the deeps.

"I take it that they're not planets after all?" Mexone asked.

"I don't what they are," the Amazon said, irritated. "They don't respond to any known test used for planets."

"There's one test you could try," Viona commented, thinking. "Color-vibration. There are four distinct colors there—ruby red, sapphire, gold, and emerald green."

"And what good would a color test do?" Abna asked politely, at which the girl shrugged.

"I haven't the faintest idea. Just a sort of hunch I've got. Just a feeling that I'd like to be sure those *are* colors, and not something else."

The Amazon hesitated, obviously not at all sure that Viona knew what she was talking about, then with a shrug she turned to the spectrometer and switched it on. In silence the four watched the readings gradually assemble themselves on the grading scale. They gave the exact wavelengths for the known colors of sapphire, gold, emerald, and ruby.

"Nothing wrong there," Abna said. "Exactly what one would expect, even though they're not planets. There is the chance that they may be extremely small planetoids which, by chance, have fallen into a mathematical design."

Viona glanced at him, obviously dissatisfied with his theory. Finally she examined the instrument carefully, then pressed one of the countless operating buttons. In consequence all the wavelengths became visible at the same time, a riot of colors. Yet at the same time they assumed a different pattern on the reproducing screen. Each distinct spectrum formed the branches of an 'X,' with the exact cross in the center cut out in a small circle of blackness.

"That's queer," the Amazon commented, musing. "I never saw a spectrometer design like that before! What did you do, Viona?"

"I switched in the multiple field," the girl said. "Normally, that would have given all the spectra in a straight line; but instead it comes out as an X. And there's certainly nothing wrong with the instrument."

Abna looked intently at the dark circle in the X's crosspiece.

"The radiations of color go that far and no further," he murmured at length. "Seems as though it might be something mathematical after all."

Mexone, who had been standing by the window in the last few moments, suddenly gave an exclamation.

"I may be wrong," he said, "but I think we're right on top of that diamond formation. It's not nearly so far away as you'd think—"

The Amazon took one look out of the window, and then gave a start of alarm. In the past few minutes the distance to the diamond formation had narrowed enormously. They were no longer distinct blazing points in directly opposite positions: they were titanic balls of gold, green, red and blue fire already bathing the *Ultra* in their unholy radiance.

"Something's wrong," Abna said curtly. "We haven't altered our speed: it's those infernal points that have come closer—"

Even as he spoke he was leaping to the switchboard,

intent on bringing the *Ultra* to a standstill as fast as possible. Even as he did so he knew this was an impossible task for the simple reason that the ship would take as long to slow down as it had to pick up speed. True, its velocity was not very great, but even then—

"Nothing you can do, Abna," the Amazon said, as he closed the switches on the panel. "We're heading right into this lot, and from the look of things we'd better be prepared for almost anything."

"And whatever this lot is, it's got us tied up in knots," Abna said grimly, looking at the instruments. "The *Ultra* isn't responding to the controls!"

"What?" The Amazon stared at him in dismay. He nodded to the switchboard.

"Look for yourself! Power is changed from thrust to recoil, and we should also be moving sideways to our former course. From these readings neither seems to be happening."

Abna was right. The view through the window confirmed it. The *Ultra* was still moving straight on, shifting neither right nor left—straight into the dark circle that now lay directly ahead. To either side, and above and below, blazed the incomprehensible color-stars.

"Magnetism," Viona said, after a moment. "That's what it must be. Some kind of magnetism."

"You're probably right," the Amazon admitted, her face a mass of conflicting hues in the weird light through the window. "But what kind of magnetism is it that can control a multi-ton mass like the *Ultra*, and set at naught its course and speed?"

None of the others attempted to answer the question. It was the first time in their experience that they had come up against a force powerful enough to control the movements of the *Ultra*; and naturally it gave them an insight as to the kind of minds that must be in control. Somewhere here, in the mystical dark of the diamond-formation's core, great intelligence was at work.

Within mere seconds, as it seemed, the *Ultra* had passed the positions of the four different colored stars and was sailing beyond them, into the dark circle which showed even against the utter black of space. At the same time the four Crusaders felt a curious sensation stealing upon them. Perhaps electrical, perhaps hypnotic: they could not be sure. There was an intense conviction of unreality, as though they were dissociated from all these happenings—and yet still a part of them. It was the most paradoxical sensation they had ever known. And, gradually, as they stood by the window trying to figure things out, there came a physical interpretation of their sensations.

The *Ultra* was becoming misty, like a thing of cloudy glass. First it was the innumerable instruments that blurred, and then the effect spread to the walls and floor. Astounded, the four realized that they could see right through the incredibly hard metal into space itself beyond.

The Amazon started to say something, and then checked herself. Sheer amazement literally snatched the words out of her mouth... There wasn't an *Ultra* anymore! It was gone. Instead, she, Abna, Viona, and Mexone were standing in a mystified group on a flawlessly laid golden floor which seemed to spread in perspective to infinity. No void, no airless vacuum—perfectly normal air to breathe. And everywhere the floor—sectionless, polished like a mirror, with a backdrop of magnificent ruby and purple color at its extremity.

It was like the biggest ballroom floor ever thought of. It was like something out of another time or dimension. It was like—

"Where the devil are we?" Abna exclaimed finally, astounded.

"Hyperspace maybe," the Amazon answered, but there was puzzlement in her violet eyes. She amended her observation and said, "I've not the least idea. Somehow we've been transported out of space to somewhere planetary and solid, but how it was done beats me."

"We're without the *Ultra*," Mexone said anxiously. "That's a point very much in our disfavor."

"We've been without it before," Viona said. "Somehow we always managed to find it again—"

She broke off as a voice suddenly spoke. It was an arresting, sharp-edged voice, booming and rolling out of the emptiness.

"Cosmic Crusaders, greetings! Do not waste your time trying to work things out because that will be beyond you. You are in the hands of those whose intelligence is vastly greater than yours."

The four looked at each other, each recognizing a scientific fact. They were no longer in space but on a planet of sorts: the voice proved it. Since it could be heard they were in atmosphere and not in space. Nevertheless four hands slid to proton guns in readiness for any emergency.

"You waste your time fingering weapons that can avail you nothing," the voice resumed, with sour derision. "To us, such antics are absurd. They are akin to what you would think if you saw an Earth baby playing with a peashooter in readiness to defend himself... Crusaders, you are powerless, and alone. But we would have speech with you— You are commanded to march—straight ahead."

A thought passed through the Amazon's mind. She had noticed that when the voice said she and the others were powerless she really felt that it *was* so. Somewhere there had to be a psychological explanation for such a conviction, but there was not the time now to look for it.

So she began walking ahead, still with her hand on her gun, the muscles on her perfect body rippling at each step she took, the weird frontal light of ruby and purple lending a weird hue to her yellow-skinned face... Abna dropped into step beside her, and Viona and Mexone brought up the rear. Not one of them was afraid, they had been through too much in the past to be that, but they certainly mystified.

"What do you, make of it?" Abna asked, as they marched across the interminable floor. "What have we dropped into this time?"

"Something basically hypnotic," the Amazon murmured. "That is all most of this is, I think. But at least we seem to be in touch with somebody who knows our language and all about us so we shan't need to educate him beforehand, as we usually do."

Abna looked about him. "I can't make out whether this is a planet, a platform in space provided with air, or what… And how long do you suppose we'll have to walk? The distance of this floor seems to be infinite."

In this, Abna was certainly correct. Two hours walking did however finally bring a change. The floor took a steep upward gradient and then resolved into colossal steps reaching up into the crazy ruby and purple glory. It looked like a magnificent sunset; it looked like Paradise; it looked like a deadly deception of Hell. Yet it had that curious unreality about it, as though it were something seen without pretending any real existence.

"In our travels," Abna said, as he and the Amazon strode up the steps side by side, "we've come up against powers which have the mastery of mental magic—but we haven't struck anything on such a grand level as this."

"Nor anything that seemed so—unconvincing," the Amazon said. "It's like trying to believe something that isn't really there. Like trying to picture a candle lighted when the flame's been blown out."

"I believe and yet disbelieve," Viona said, lower down the steps.

"A dream with all the power of reality," Mexone added. "Like dreaming of a thing and telling yourself it is a dream. A dream within a dream..."

Purposeless words. The desperate struggle of trained minds to come to grips with something impossible. Such statements were the safety valves by which the Crusaders released their baffled emotions... And presently they reached the top of the steps and there stopped, stunned by the eye-wrenching magnificence of the view before them.

There were steps leading downwards from the eminence on which they now stood, steps identical to those up which they had come. There were twenty of them in all, debouching into yet another room, or plain—or something—filled with all manner of weird machines and bathed in the curious ruby-purple light. This latter seemed to be coming from a single blazing ball hanging in the sky, the air—or something, and having no visible means of support.

"No people—no anything," Abna said at last, taking a deep breath. "No walls, no roof. Is it a room or an external plain of some kind?"

"External plain, I should think. I get the impression that we're on a planet with a perpetually calm climate, therefore everything is laid out in the open..."

"You are correct, Golden Amazon of Earth," confirmed the sharp-edged voice—and at the same tine as the words were uttered a distant green light bobbed in and out. A light atop a tower of latticed metal and having a multitude of wires connected to it.

"So that's where the voice is coming from," the Amazon muttered. "And presumably hidden mikes are picking up our voices."

"And hidden telecameras reflecting our actions," Viona added, peering over her mother's shoulder with wonder in her blue eyes.

"Advance, Crusaders!" commanded the voice, after a moment. "Advance to the tower with the green light—which I gather you have already seen."

The four obeyed, drawn on by interest and not therefore feeling particularly afraid. They descended the twenty mighty steps and then walked through the midst of the incredible machines, trying—and failing—to analyze them as they went. The fact remained that there was nothing comprehensible.

They stopped finally perhaps two yards from the tower with the green light and stood looking up at it. It was perhaps a hundred foot high, not unlike a very delicately constructed lighthouse. At the base of it, imprisoned amongst the girders, was a four-sided enclosure that could have passed for a control room of sorts… But nowhere were there any people.

The Amazon's attention strayed from the colorful perplexity to the sky. For a moment she caught a glimpse of a star—a genuine star. Then another. That satisfied her. This then, was a planet of sorts, but the most bizarre one she and the others had ever encountered.

"You are interesting beings," said the voice at length, and the green light winked with the pulsation of the words. "I have been examining you carefully, internally and externally, and although, you are wonderfully fashioned after your kind, you are still very low in the scale of intelligence."

The Amazon smiled cynically. "We have heard that comment from others besides you, my friend—and we have lived to prove the statement wrong."

"That I do not doubt—but as yet you have not encountered a race like ours, a race evolved into pure mental expression, a race so complete that it is all one, centered into the solitary being who is addressing you, now. We—I—am the race."

"We have heard of such happenings," the Amazon said, still in the same sardonic tone. "A race merged into one being. It is not beyond possibility."

"Obviously. We have done it. But we are not the mergence of bodies, but of minds. All the minds of the race—our greatest thinkers—are pooled as one. And as one we—I—speak."

"You are to be congratulated," the Amazon said, watching the tower intently. "Your accomplishment seems to suggest it is rather futile to wish to converse with such as us—lowly beings from a faraway planetary system."

"I converse with you because you are the Cosmic Crusaders."

"What has that to do with it?" Abna asked bluntly.

"Everything! Is not your aim and purpose to confer scientific knowledge and uplift on those peoples who are ignorant? Do you not interfere with planets and their peoples under the pretext of conferring ever-lasting benefit?"

"We never interfere," the Amazon snapped. "Our scientific and physical powers are used only to help those who need help. What interference we have made has been with those people, or groups of people, who have tried ruthlessly to dominate. Wherever we find that issue arising we will crush it."

"By what right?" asked the sharp-edged voice, coldly. "By what right do you dare to assume that your standards are the correct ones?"

"In the Universe there are only two powers," Abna said. "One is real and it is called 'Right.' The other is unreal and is a complete illusion. It is called 'Wrong,' or more generally 'Evil.' By that we set our standard. When there is only right which makes sense or has any lasting quality it is our job to bestow it or foster it in every way we can."

"Abna of Jupiter, you are a fool!" the voice sneered. "So too is your wife, and your daughter... And this Mexone of a far-off world. The two powers of the Universe are always at war with each other, and which-ever has the greater preponderance of power wins... We believe equally in right and wrong, not disparaging one or the other, merely obeying whichever seems the most likely to provide advancement. We have watched you very closely, my friends, throughout your experiences since you first came to this Galaxy. And we have not been impressed with your activities."

The four remained silent, though their expressions

clearly showed their resentment.

"It has been a long story of interference in the rights of those who had magnificent plans for the furtherance of scientific power throughout the universe. Every time you have destroyed those dreams, deposed those who had the power and the knowledge and given freedom to the little-minded fools who will be eons before they amount to anything. You have left behind you, in your various adventures, a chain of semi-intelligent halfwits, when there could have been a magnificent scientific interstellar empire! You have even destroyed worlds to further your so-called standards! Kolb was the latest world you destroyed. Races and individuals you have also destroyed with your fantastic weapon, the zero-quantity amplifier."

The Amazon gave Abna a glance. The mention of the zero-quantity amplifier gave her real cause for worry. It was a fabulous instrument, capable of destroying any known form of matter on the basis of matter being of a lower grade than amplified thought. Nobody must ever know its secret or the dreadful power it could wield.

"Summing up," the voice continued. "We decided that your activities must be curbed, and your mistaken notions destroyed, otherwise it will become impossible for any scientific race to make any progress without having you interfering… We set a trap for you and, as we hoped, curiosity drew you into it. Four circles of cosmic magnetism were set up in space in the form of a diamond-shaped opening. The waves from them hid the planet beyond—*this* planet. Your *Ultra* ran into the trap and was dissolved by mental force, but you were preserved to come here and answer for yourselves."

"Much that you have said, I do not believe," the Amazon said, after a long pause. "You convey the impression of mighty power, and yet I think most of it is clever illusion. You are handling our minds to an extraordinary degree, but once we get the hang of it we'll react—violently."

"There will not be time for you to react, Golden Amazon. You, and these others stand accused as unnecessary elements in this region of space—as barriers to scientific advancement in general and our own plans in particular. Therefore it is agreed that we destroy you, as completely and absolutely as we have destroyed your space machine."

Instead of saying anything the Amazon acted— suddenly. She whipped out her proton gun and sighted it on the glowing green light on the tower. A second later the gun was torn out of her hand and an invisible blow sent her crashing to the polished floor. For a second or two she lay there, half stunned; then Abna moved over and helped her to her feet.

"Not a very enterprising action, Amazon," the voice said. "If it has done nothing else, it has at least shown you that hostility against us is a completely wasted thing."

The Amazon breathed hard, but she did not say anything. There was a cold glitter in her eyes.

"To resume..." the voice continued, as though nothing had happened. "Your activities, as I said before, must be curbed. But before you leave there is one secret which I—we—must have: the secret of the zero-quantity amplifier."

"You'll not have that secret—ever," the Amazon retorted. "In any case, there is no reason why you should need it. With your complete mastery of mind, so you, say, you cannot possibly be interested in a machine which deals solely with matter."

"I will decide where my interests lie, Amazon! The secret—now!"

The Amazon set her mouth tightly, and the same stubborn look came to the faces of the others. A few second passed, then the green light bobbed again as the voice resumed.

"Very well. You compel me to use persuasion. I know it would be difficult to break either you, Amazon, or you, Abna. But it will be interesting to see bow you react to watching your daughter Viona in the grip of lethal forces… Like this!"

Again the mysterious force that had felled the Amazon to the floor went into action. Before any moves could be made Viona was picked up invisibly and then hurled with savage force for a distance of several yards. She hit the polished floor with vicious impact, but before she had time to recover the unknown something was at work again, driving into every portion of her body, stabbing her with invisible harpoons of what felt like electrical energy. Viona was strong, immensely so, but even she could not help crying out in anguish as the onslaught continued.

For a moment or two the Amazon stared at her writhing body and listened to her agonized cries; then with Abna and Mexone beside her she catapulted forward— To be brought to a standstill by a solid wall which could be felt and not seen. She rubbed her bruised shoulder painfully and swung to look at the green light.

"Don't waste your time, my friends," the voice said. "I purposely cast Viona to a distance so that a barrier could be placed between you and her... Are you going to tell me what I wish to know, or shall I exterminate Viona before your very eyes?"

And to amplify his statement the being, presence, or whatever he was, suddenly increased the fury of his attack on Viona. Utterly helpless against it, nearly fainting with the pain of outraged nerves, Viona screamed frantically.

"Stop!" the Amazon commanded, her fists clenched. "Stop it! Let her alone. I'll tell you what you wish to know."

"Very sensible of you, Amazon. Very well: I will keep my part of the bargain."

For Viona, the anguish abruptly ceased. She was lifted, limp and shivering, in the unknown power and flung like a rag doll at the feet of Abna. Instantly he went down and gathered her shaking body in his arms.

"Speak, Amazon! I am waiting!"

The Amazon withdrew her gaze from Viona and turned to the green light. It gleamed like the solitary eye of a Gorgon, implacable, emerald. She began relating the details of the zero-quantity formula, giving every detail of it. When she had finished she relaxed into a stony calmness.

"You are to be congratulated," the voice commented. "I can see from the formula that the device is one using negative thought at the power of zero, by which material formation ceases to exist. Excellent! Such a formula will be valuable indeed."

"If you hadn't destroyed the *Ultra* you would have had the zero-quantity machine there, ready for use," the Amazon remarked bitterly.

"Maybe so, but to have a machine before you and not know how it operates is rather useless, do you not think? I prefer to know the how and the why, Amazon…"

There was silence for a moment. Viona struggled to her feet with her father's great arm around her. She still looked shaken, but otherwise was practically recovered. Mexone moved to her side, and glared malignantly at the green light.

"You've got the whip-hand of us at the moment," he said, "but someday you're going to pay for the way you attacked Viona! You'll not get away with it, believe me."

For answer there was a sudden whirring sound; then before Mexone, Abna, or Viona could do a thing they found their weapon belts had been stripped from them and flung several feet away. The Amazon, already divested of her gun, felt at her belt with its remaining weapons and tools—and that too was whipped off and flung on one side.

"You are safer without weapons, my friends," the voice said. "If you doubt it, recall the Amazon's attempted attack on me a little while ago… It is better that you go out into space—that space from which you have come—without weapons, without provisions, and—without hope. There could be no better way to make you pay the price of interference. Quick death in a dozen different ways is not for such as you. You must have some time to think before you die—some time in which to realize that you are not such mighty beings as you think…"

CHAPTER 2

THE RED PLANET

For a moment there was silence. The quartet looked at each other, wondering what was intended—then they gave a start as the mental powers, or magical processes, of their sadistic captor again became evident...guided by invisible forces four cylindrical objects came gliding into view, each one equipped with the unmistakable outlines of rocket exhaust fins.

"Space machines!" the Amazon exclaimed, in spite of herself, as the four objects glided to a standstill on the immense floor a little distance away.

"Yes, space machines," agreed the voice. "Each one capable of holding one person, of your physical size and shape. I would point out that they are one-way machines, and by reason of being securely imprisoned within them, you will have no way of controlling them. They will travel space continuously until drawn aside by the gravitation of a star or a planet, then they will crash. Between that time and this each one of you will have time to reflect—individually and out of touch with each other—on what it means to interfere with the plans of scientists who are no concern of yours."

"There is one thing you haven't explained," the Amazon said. "You speak constantly of our interference. That statement is completely untrue, but even assuming it to be correct why should you be concerned about it? We have not interfered with anything you are doing: why set yourself up as judge for scientists who don't mean a thing to you?"

"We do not feel disposed to answer your question, Amazon."

"That I can well believe," the Amazon snapped. "You are planning something big, which our presence might interfere with—hence you wish to be rid of us. Others have tried to be rid of us, remember, and accomplished nothing."

"What others hove done is no concern of ours: we do not make mistakes, ever! As for our planning something— Well, perhaps. Do not scientists always plan ahead?"

The Amazon remained silent, thinking out something to herself. Abna, Mexone, and Viona grouped around her, waiting. Then the voice resumed:

"Time enough has been wasted. You will enter those space machines— And as a matter of courtesy you are informed that beyond this planet there is mainly empty space. Only one world might give you trouble if you fall into its gravitation. Beyond that there is the void, for light years ahead. You love the void, my friends, and you shall have it—as your burial ground."

To attempt resistance was naturally useless; and in

any case the four found themselves suddenly in the relentless forces with which this weird planet seemed to be infested. Unable to help themselves they were impelled towards the four space machines.

"As you hurtle through space to your final extinction, think of us—the Lords of Creation!" the voice said. "By no other name will you remember us..."

There was no chance to make a comment: even less to ask a question. Frantically though they fought, with every vestige of their superhuman strength, the four were each forced into one of the spaceships—and still under muscular compulsion were compelled to lie face downwards on a narrow metal floor. There was just room, and no more.

The Amazon fought more desperately than anybody, but even her great strength was insufficient to overcome the irresistible force that dragged her arms up in front of her head, and then clamped her wrists to the floor with metal manacles. She felt the same thing happen to her ankles. Yet another band—or rather a half-hoop—of metal snapped into place about her waist. Then the power relaxed but she could hardly budge a fraction of an inch. At least she was warm from the radiation of hidden heaters.

She listened, her body cramped and strained to the uttermost. The entranceway through which she had been forced suddenly went dark as an airlock door shut. Machinery hummed somewhere behind her feet, then from her sensations she judged that the tiny ship in which she was imprisoned was hurtling upwards...

Deadly sickness came over her at the numbing drag of acceleration; and it was a sickness that lasted until the machine was free of the gravitational drag of the mystery planet. Only then did a semblance of normalcy return to her, and with it returned the awareness of stretched muscles and mercilessly cramped limbs.

The machinery somewhere behind her feet clicked suddenly and then became silent as automatic means presumably controlled it. Everything was quiet— horribly quiet. The utter silence that could only be the void.

The Amazon forced up her head, lifting her face from the icy cold metal against which it was pressed. Ahead of her she could see her extended arms drawn taut, the manacles across her wrists. Beyond her hands was the nose of the ship, and inlet into it was a small curved window, which gave her a view of space. Black, abysmal, except for remote smudges of nebulous light, which she realized were island universes countless light-centuries distant— But no, there was something else. To the extreme right, as the ship slightly altered course, she beheld a dull red disk, definitely a planet, and not unlike Mars in appearance. This was evidently the solitary world of which the voice had spoken. Certainly there was no other planet or star in sight—or at least within measurable distance.

With a sudden jerk the Amazon strained her wrists and arms to the full extent of her strength. Immediately the sharp edges of the wrist manacles dug into her flesh and left bleeding cuts as she relaxed again. She breathed hard, trying not to believe the grim truth that she was for once in a prison from which her colossal strength could not release her.

For a long time she lay quiet, her face against the cold metal, trying to reason a way out of the situation. Other thoughts came into her mind, too. Presumably Viona, Abna, and Mexone were also in a plight like hers, utterly trapped, hurtling through space, to eventual extinction… Lords of Creation? What had the voice meant by that? It implied a lot to the Amazon but she had not the time to concentrate freely at the moment. Later, when she had freed herself, perhaps…

At last she raised her head again, to behold the unknown red planet a good deal nearer. Evidently the tiny ship was traveling at a fair velocity, even though she was not conscious of it. If it kept on a straight course towards that planet, drawn by its gravitational field, a final collision with it was inevitable… That spurred her again to savage physical movement. Wrists and ankles were drawn taut against the manacles; she even tried to arch her back against the hoop imprisoning her waist. All to no purpose. She relaxed again at last, her wrists and ankles savagely cut, her emotions close to panic.

Minutes passed. The strain of being stretched out flat was commencing to make itself felt. Little barbs of pain were creeping up her thighs and along her arms. Breathing hard, she raised her face again to look through the window and estimate the distance of the red planet. It was slightly nearer—but there was something else which riveted the Amazon's attention, something nearly unbelievable. There was Abna, in space, gliding slowly towards her, his arms extended over his head like a diver about to plunge into the deep end.

"Dreams!" the Amazon whispered, shaking the tumbled blonde hair out of her eyes. "It can't be Abna—"

But it definitely was! He was moving through space in a straight line, kicking his legs now and again in thrusting motion, obviously trying to give himself recoil. For the rest, he seemed to be relying on the infinitesimal gravity of the Amazon's spaceship to draw him to it... And within seconds, it did! As the bewildered Amazon heard the thud of his body striking the outside of the space machine she knew then it was not a dream: instead it was perhaps a miracle.

She relaxed again, her face to the metal floor. She listened intently, trying to ignore the murderous cramp that was plaguing her. Then at last there came a clanking sound, and with it the air-pressure in the ship dropped abruptly. It whistled and screeched as it escaped into the vacuum of outer space. But only for a moment as the airlock door closed again... The Amazon jerked her face up, just as Abna struggled into a lying position, beside her.

"Not too much room, is there?" he asked, with that dryness which was his wont on occasions.

"How did you get here?" the Amazon demanded, screwing her head round to look at him.

"I'll tell you in a moment. Right now I'd better get you and the others free. It's as I've always said: if you really get into something you can't master, come to me."

"All right, so I'm beaten!" the Amazon retorted. "But only because you got here so quickly. Given time, I'd have freed myself."

"Perhaps…" Abna was working swiftly on the manacles. "I don't think you'd have got out of this mess in a month of Sundays if it hadn't been for me—and metaphysics."

He snapped open the wrist manacles, bending the self-actuating metal catch which held them. The Amazon slowly began to move her arms, then stopped again until Abna released her ankles and waist. Even then she could hardly move.

"I've things to do—and quickly," Abna said, glancing through the window. "That red planet is dangerously near—"

The Amazon muttered something as she winced under the pins and needles of returning circulation. Abna, crouched, hauled her into a sitting position, the most he could do in such cramped quarters.

"I'm going to release Viona and Mexone," he said, effecting not to notice a faint indignation on the Amazon's face. "You just sit there and massage some life back into yourself. I've got to hurry." And he scrambled over her legs to the airlock.

"But how did you survive out there, without air and in the zero conditions of space?" the Amazon questioned, staring after him.

"All a matter of metaphysical power, which I don't

often use. I'll explain later. I'll have to drop your air pressure, I'm afraid, whilst I escape. Meantime, figure out how to reverse the power on this rocket ship from thrust to recoil. Only way with that red planet claiming us."

With that Abna was on his way. Once again the precious air sang and hissed as he briefly opened the lock; then he had closed it behind him. Struggling to the window, the Amazon saw him floating diver-wise across the airless gap between her own space machine and the accompanying three other vessels.

She reflected for a moment. She understood part of the miracle, but not all of it. Abna himself would have to fill in the gaps—and in any case she had immediate problems of her own to deal with. Abna had said something about reversing the power of the little machine from thrust to recoil—thereby, presumably, firing it away from the planet towards which it was headed, or at least making its impact with that world comparatively gentle.

The Amazon had not the kind of temperament to take orders, but this time she knew they made sense. She knew too that Abna had spoken the truth: reversal of power was all that could stop a head-on smash to destruction—so she turned around in the narrow space and started a careful examination of the ship's motive power. The first thing she discovered was that it was all automatic, and using some kind of liquid fuel which she had never encountered before. There seemed to be precious little of it, too.

The more she studied the engine the more she realized the impossibility of doing anything to reverse it. Then as she crouched there trying to figure the problem out she became aware that something was happening to the ship itself. It was turning slowly round in a half circle! It seemed to be performing the maneuver in a series of jerks, and before each jerk there came a thud, as though something were forcibly striking the machine's outer hull.

Once again the Amazon struggled to the window and peered outside. She stared in amazement at the vision of Abna jumping—literally jumping—against the ship and then receding to a slight distance in space as the recoil flung him away, only to be chained again by the vessel's minute attraction which dragged him back—to the accompaniment of yet another jump. And at each jump the vessel swung further round.

The Amazon looked at the other ships. Two of them were now flying in reverse. The third one, presumably Abna's, was front-way round as it had always been. A jerk, and now the Amazon's machine was back to front. A few seconds later the airlock opened and shut. The air pressure dropped so low it made breathing a real difficulty.

Then Abna, his face a hard mask of concentration, struggled over to the automatic rocket-engine, made a few adjustments, and then started it into action. Outside, the rockets flared with life, projection now towards the somber red world in the depths of space.

"What's going on?" the Amazon demanded, as Abna

crawled over to her. "What's this all about?"

"Merely a repetition of something you once did with a missile headed for Earth, Vi. You turned it round in space by jumping against its nose: surely you remember? The gravity presented by the mass of the ship is just enough to keep you floating away entirely... That is all I have done. We can now fire the rockets against this red world and prevent ourselves crashing. I told the others to fire their engines when I started ours—I see they've done it," Abna added, squinting through the window.

"I can understand you forcing the ships round since in space they have no appreciable weight," the Amazon said. "But I still don't understand how you've done everything else— Did you say something about metaphysics?"

"I did." Abna's face had become serious. "One of the longest spells of devout concentration I've ever attempted, but though I haven't indulged in metaphysics for a long time it's obvious that I haven't lost my touch."

"Very obvious. Nothing else could explain away your surviving in the void like that. I know a human body retains its warmth and air for a few minutes in the airless void, but you—"

"Mind, Vi. The stronger power. I used it to the full to get out of an otherwise impossible situation. Metaphysics were never much in your line, were they?"

The Amazon said: "I believe in them, but I'm a poor demonstrator. I admit that you're the master in that province."

"I concentrated until this material being you call Abna became entirely subservient to mental power," Abna explained. "I did it once before between planets, if you remember, to save myself from so-called death. I could do it this time because there was absolute peace, which did not disturb my concentration… Once in that state the material body mattered no more. I passed through the manacles; I had the intelligence to work out the formula of the airlock's automatic fastenings; I was able to move in space in perfect freedom, separated—as long as I kept my concentration free—from all material trammels. I released you, Viona, and Mexone. I turned the ships round and now…"

Abna looked through the window onto the growing red world. "And now I am Abna again, a trifle exhausted by the mental exercise through which I put myself."

The Amazon looked at him for a moment and then said rather irrelevantly, "I wonder if the mystics of Tibet, who walk through flames unburned, or some of the Biblical characters of old, had some glimpse of the metaphysical power which you use so well?"

"Possible—in fact probable." Abna stirred a little in the cramped space and looked at the Amazon's wrists and ankles, still cut and bloodstained where the material of her tights had been ripped away.

"I'm all right," she said quietly, analyzing his thoughts. "Nothing that won't heal very quickly… Let's face the immediate problem, Abna. What are we going to do when we hit that red world—as inevitably we will?"

"I don't know until we get there. The interesting point, to my mind, is that the Lords of Creation—as the green light called himself and his race—evidently did not anticipate that we'd land on that planet and survive. We nay learn quite a lot by doing that."

The Amazon nodded and then, by dint of pressing her face close to the window glass, looked back at the planet from which they had been hurled. It loomed as a dark circle against space itself, surrounded by the curious diamond formation, the light of which was still casting across space like a weak multicolored sun.

"I just cannot understand what the Lords of Creation intend to do," the Amazon said at last. "I had thought of the usual thing—domination of neighbor worlds, but there are none within a reasonable radius. Sometimes I think—"

Whatever was in her mind was not spoken for at that moment the tiny vessel obviously increased its velocity as it fell into the real core of the red planet's attraction. Abna tightened his lips as he gazed through the window.

"This is it!" he said grimly. "We'll find out the hard way whether these rockets have enough thrust to keep us from smashing ourselves up! Hang on!"

The Amazon nodded tensely but she did not speak. Within the last thirty minutes the space machine had covered a huge distance, drawn by the constant pull of the red planet. Now it was the final plunge—and for the other two rockets containing Viona and Mexone.

The jets flaring, and exerting a cushioning force, all three ships screamed downwards from outer space and presently struck the red planet's atmospheric layer. Noticeably, speed slackened. The jets and the, air resistance together formed an extremely useful brake.

Down the machines swept—and still down, through layers of cloud so dense they amounted to fog. The further the descent the more the weak multicolored 'sunlight' began to fade, until in the last two hundred miles light had gone altogether. For the anxiously watching quartet the windows were blankly dark.

Abna's great hand stole out of the blackness and closed over the Anazon's in a reassuring grip. She looked at him quickly—or at least endeavored to do so. She met only a wall of blackness. And outside, the scream of the riven atmosphere.

Faster—yet faster—into an abyss of a world. Then suddenly an overwhelming shock as speed stopped dead. The Amazon felt her head smash against hard metalwork while around her there was a chaos of sound as metallic bars splintered under the force of an unholy concussion…

* * * *

A head with immensely broad shoulders loomed gradually on the Amazon's clearing vision. Behind the head and shoulders low cloud was drifting like smoke, painted from below with a pulsating crimson that seemed to suggest a vast fire of some kind.

The Amazon stirred very gently. She was conscious

of no aches and pains: rather indeed of a feeling of well-being. By degrees she realized she was lying on her back on rocky ground. Abna was bending over her, and some little distance away Viona and Mexone were seated on a rock spur, gazing rather dispiritedly about them in the red glow.

"Better?" Abna asked quietly, and the Amazon nodded. Then she looked surprised.

"Better? There wasn't anything wrong with me. I remember we crashed, that I hit my head against the wall—"

"And broke your neck," Abna finished. "Also an arm. I was more fortunate and got free." He gave a sigh of relief. "As a matter of interest, Vi, you've been clinically dead for two hours."

"Dead? But—" The Amazon suddenly relaxed and smiled a little. "I understand! You've been busy with your metaphysics again?"

"No other way to restore you. Viona and Mexone were pretty badly knocked about too, but they're okay now. Here we are, all fit and smiling, on a world that looks as though it's been spawned out of an inferno."

The Amazon got to her feet as Abna assisted her. Viona and Mexone came over to join them. In silence they all surveyed the lowering, ominous clouds with their flame-tinting. This indeed was the only light that reached them.

It was a depressing scene. As far as they could see there was nothing but desolate rock—not the remotest suggestion of grass or vegetation of any kind. And out of the cloud-wreathed blackness there came a constant hissing and rumbling that bespoke deep volcanic power.

"From what little I've seen of this world," Abna said at length, "it looks like parts of Jupiter, my home planet. The only difference is that the gravity is comparatively normal and the air quite breathable. As for light: I don't think there is any except the reflection from volcanic fire, such as we see on those clouds."

"Is there a crater of some kind over there?" the Amazon asked, nodding towards the red glare.

"Yes." Abna nodded somberly. "I've been that far. There seems be a huge line of boiling metal that bars our path if we want to go in that direction. Not that I can think why we should want to, anyway."

"Equally," Viona said, "we can't just stand here and do nothing. We've no food, no water—"

"No weapons," Mexone put in grimly.

"And no spaceships," the Amazon concluded, glancing towards three battered hulks which had crashed into the rockery. Where the fourth machine was—the one that had not been turned round—none of them knew. Having hit this satanic planet with no recoil jets to save it, it had probably been burned up or smashed to powder.

Abna said, "There might be something amongst the ruins of those spaceships which we could retrieve."

Nobody said anything. All of four of them were just commencing to realize the kind of spot they were in. Usually they could see a loophole in a desperate situation, but this time there did not appear to be one.

"Let's try moving to somewhere a little safer," the Amazon said finally. "I have the uncomfortable feeling that that crater ahead of us may explode at any moment, and that would be the finish. You never know what we might come across."

She began moving into the sulfuric smoke wreaths with Abna by her side and Viona and Mexone bringing up the rear. They paused for a moment to dubiously survey the wrecks of the space machines as they passed them; then went on again. The immediate problem to all of them was hunger and thirst, just commencing to make insistent demands.

Gradually, as they moved, the red light cast by the volcanic fire began to wane, shading into a deep twilight. Overhead there were heavy clouds, heavy enough to prevent any starlight getting through, and otherwise there was no form of illumination whatever. The twilight, such as it was, must be coming from the faint light cast by the planet they had left—that and the multicolored balls of magnetism which surrounded it.

In time the red glare died altogether. The Amazon dragged to a stops struck by a thought.

"Are we being foolish?" she asked, as Abna looked at her in the gloom. "We might yet convert those wrecked spaceships somehow, but we'll never do it if we can't find them again. We're getting further and further from them."

"True enough." Abna considered this for a moment, then an idea seemed to occur to him. "Wait here a moment, Vi. "I'll fix it."

He retreated into the darkness and slowly vanished from sight. After perhaps ten minutes he came back, paying out behind him a long whitish thread from a bundle in his hand. As he came up he explained.

"A thread of my uniform," he said. "It will unravel as we advance, and with the other end fastened to the space ship wrecks we can't miss."

The Amazon smiled a little at the astonishing simplicity of the idea, and as she well knew there were miles of tough silver-nylon fiber in the sleeveless waistcoat-like garment of which Abna had now divested himself. Certainly he did not feel its loss since the air was volcanically warm... So progress resumed, Abna still paying out the thread from the garment in his hand.

What the four hoped to accomplish by thus probing the gloom of this empty, rocky world they did not know. The main urge was to move from the volcanic area and, perhaps, they might even come to a region where rock ceased and vegetation began, thereby providing a possibility of satisfying their hunger and thirst. Silently they argued to themselves that a space traveler landing on Earth in the arid dryness of the Sahara might well believe that the whole Earth was made up of sand— unaware of the amenities no great distance away. So it might be here. They had had no chance to survey the planet telescopically before crashing onto it.

But the passage of time seemed to give the lie to their hopes. The rocky scenery remained unchanged, and there was only the dim twilight glow in which to find their way about. At last they came to a halt, tired and depressed. They sat down on the rocks and surveyed.

"Isn't there something you can do, Abna?" the Amazon demanded at length. "Metaphysically, perhaps? After that effort in space, this surely shouldn't be beyond you?"

He meditated for a moment and then sighed. "I'm afraid it is, Vi. I could overcome the difficulties for myself alone—as I did out in space—but to do it for three others at the same time would prove too much of an effort. There are limits sometimes, even to metaphysical power."

Long silence, as four minds groped with difficulty. Then it was Viona who spoke, her tone wondering,

"Look at that over there! What is it? Water?"

The others looked, and after a moment saw what she meant. In a nearby recess of the rocks something strange was evident, something that was reflecting the rockery in a mirror-like fashion. Puzzled, Abna got to his feet and went over to examine the phenomenon. In a matter of moments he knew that Viona's guess had been correct: there *was* water, quite a considerable pool of it. Nor was it the only one. There were quite a few pools scattered about in the rocks.

Abna didn't waste any time considering the pros and cons. He dipped his finger in the pool and then licked his finger. The moisture was delightful to lips and mouth dry with thirst, and except for a strong saline quality the water seemed more or less pure... Abna didn't need to call the others: they had been watching his actions, and without further ado—regardless of consequences—they drank their fill. Then they looked at each other.

"If there are after effects we'll chance them," Viona said, shrugging. "Anyway, with our thirst slaked we can still last out a long time without food."

"True enough," the Amazon agreed, "but food we have got to get from somewhere…"

"I wonder," Abna said, pondering, "how this water got here in the first place? There are no signs of an underground river or stream that might explain it, and rain doesn't seem to be a common occurrence on this planet. Yet we have these pools, and considerable sized ones at that—"

He seemed about to say something more, but was interrupted by a bass roaring in the ground—a roar that grew rapidly into a shriek and deafened the eardrums. At the same time the rocks began to quake danger-ously as though the whole area were about to explode.

"Earthquake!" Mexone shouted hoarsely. "We'd better get out of here—"

The words died in his throat as the earthquake suddenly manifested itself—in the most incredibly powerful geyser the four had ever seen. With a din like an exploding cannon a vast jet of boiling water soared up and up into the heavy clouds, steam and scalding drops cascading from it. The four gasped as the searing rain dropped on then, but it was not suffi-ciently widespread to cause them any serious injury.

They retreated to a slight distance and stood watching, awe-stricken by the power of the geyser.

"There's the explanation of the water," Abna shouted in the Amazon's ear. "Something like 'Old Faithful' way back on Earth from the look of it—only a hundred, even a thousand times more powerful."

The Amazon nodded, too interested to speak. For ten minutes the vast outburst of inner forces continued, the top of the jet wreathed in a circle of steam—then just as suddenly it ceased and there were only water pools and drifting steam to show that it had ever been.

"Very interesting," the Amazon said at last, "even if it doesn't get us anywhere."

"Don't be too sure that doesn't," Abna said slowly. "We ought to be able to use power like that somehow—"

"Look up there!" Viona interrupted, pointing. "The sky's clearing!"

It was a fact. Perhaps the heat of the geyser jet had had some kind of action on the lowering clouds, or maybe the occurrence was a natural rift in the barrier. Whatever it was, the sky was visible, purplish gray due to there being an atmosphere. The smudges of vastly distant nebulae were visible—and something else! The planet from which they had come. It loomed in full view as the clouds parted, flanked by the multicolored balls of magnetism. A dark, somber world, as cruel— they knew—as any world on which they had so far set foot.

"If I ever get back there," the Amazon muttered, staring skywards, "I've an account to settle with that green light, or whatever is behind it."

She was about to say more, and then stopped, her eye attracted by the gradual fading into appearance of a deep violet beam—and it projected from the planet of somber darkness. A beam probing into the depths of space where there were no other planets or form of cosmic matter.

"Do you suppose they're searching for us?" Abna asked, as the beam continued to project for untold millions of miles.

"I don't think so." The Amazon was thinking hard. "As far as they know we went on into space and would be beyond their range by now. No, it's something else—"

She broke off, her breath catching with shock. Simultaneously she and the others flung their hands over their eyes as, at the extreme limit of the beam— an incomprehensible distance away in space—there flared a blinding star, a sun, a core of intolerably bright light that could instantly have blinded them had they not taken such quick precaution.

And the core of liquid flame grew. And grew.

CHAPTER 3
ESCAPE INTO SPACE

Peeping through their fingers for split-second intervals the quartet was able to follow the progress of the newly created star as it kindled in the void. Then after a while its original blazing glory dimmed somewhat and they were able to watch with unshielded eyes. They watched, even if they did not understand, and they prayed at the same tine that the cloud wreaths would remain parted and not interrupt their vision.

"What would you say it is, Vi?" Abna asked, puzzled. "It looks like atomic fire of some sort—but why should the Lords of Creation want to project atomic fire into space on the end of a thrust beam—if that's what it is. It doesn't make sense."

"Perhaps it's a sun," the Amazon answered. "If an artificial one they would kindle it first as atomic fire, and afterwards it would feed itself by the breakdown of energies—as do all normal suns and stars. This system certainly needs a sun, so—"

She broke off, staring. As indeed the others were doing also. Something was happening out there in space, things without precedent in their experiences. The artificial sun was visibly gyrating like a stupendous Catherine wheel. It was no longer a ball of fire. It was a flaming mass spinning rapidly and having filaments visibly projecting from its edges, and growing larger.

"Now I get it!" Abna exclaimed suddenly, astounded. "They're creating a system of planets! We know systems of planets can be created that way—rapid revolution of the parent sun flinging off streamers of molten matter, which condense into worlds. That's what we're viewing."

Such seemed to be the case. More rays sprang from the dark world to augment the main ray. Under their influence, and within minutes of time, fragments—as they seemed to be, but actually they must have been thousands of square miles in area—were torn from the flaming mass in the heavens and hurled centrifugally to various parts of the void. It all seemed haphazard, and yet even so perfectly balanced scientific forces had at last wrested six small planets from the mother-sun, six small and flaming worlds which swept round their primary in planned orbits... The whole act of cosmic creation did not last more than an hour; in that time sun and planets were born. The rest would merely be a matter of cooling, so far as the planets were concerned, and some of the rays that were at work would hasten such a process.

Then, one by one, the rays snuffed out. The distant dark planet with its attendant moons of magnetism, was back to its former enigmatic state. Abna turned his attention from the sky and looked at the Amazon questioningly.

"Any ideas?" he asked.

"I hardly know…" The Amazon contemplated the heavens. "But—it's obvious that for some reason the Lords of Creation—as they call themselves—have established a sun and a planetary system by scientific means, out in the empty spaces where there is infinite room for a system to develop. Which proves one thing…"

"What?"

"They are not such mental wizards as they would have us believe. If, as they claim, they do most things by thought, why need they use beams and other material effects to create a solar system? Mind alone should have been sufficient for their purpose."

"Mmm—true enough," Abna admitted.

"Which also suggests that the various things they did on their own planet, like forcing us into the coffin spaceships and performing tricks which suggested mental power of the nth degree, were nothing more than tricks. That being so it's possible, by the same reckoning, that the green light being is also a trick—a supposed wizard of mental power with feet of clay."

"Yes…could be," Abna nodded slowly.

"Magicians or otherwise," Viona remarked, "they are evidently not intent on dominating some other world, or worlds—which is something of a change. They're creating, not destroying. Which makes it hard to fathom why they were so anxious to be rid of us. We would never have stopped them trying to create planets. Rather would we have upheld such a marvelous idea."

"There may have been other reasons for their wishing to be rid of us," the Amazon said thoughtfully. "Probably we'll come across them in time. At the moment we can only accept as we find."

There was a good deal more she intended to say, but she did not have the opportunity. Suddenly she and the others were trying to keep their feet in the midst of a violent earthquake. At least they assumed it was that: the only thing that puzzled them was the absence of subterranean noises, such as usually accompany any violent tremors of the ground. It was over almost as soon as it had begun and the swaying, rocky landscape returned to normal.

"The sooner we get away from this volcanic planet the better I'll like it," Viona said, glancing about her. "I don't like the thought of never knowing what's going to happen next."

"For your information, Viona, that wasn't an earthquake," Abna said. "Or at least not one of the normal sort. It was a shifting of gravitational centers, caused by the arrival of that sun and planets in outer space. Now equilibrium has been reached I don't suppose we'll be troubled again."

The Amazon smiled wryly to herself, irritated that she had not herself thought of this logical explanation. She glanced skywards towards the planets, and then sighed as she failed to discern them. The cloudy vapors had closed over again.

"All this apart," she said at length, "it's more than time that we decided what we're going to do about ourselves. All we have done is manage to find a drink. We're as far from food and any form of security as we ever were."

"Let's examine the situation," Abna said. "Primarily, we want to find out what the Lords of Creation are driving at, don't we? We want to know what they meant by having some sort of a plan?"

"We know what that is," the Amazon said. "The creation of those planets."

"But suppose that's only part of it? What if it is intended to populate those planets? Don't we want to know by what sort of people? Don't we want to warn those people that their creators are proven liars as far as mental powers are concerned?"

"I suppose so," the Amazon admitted. "But what of our own position? Doesn't that come first?"

Viona said, "Most certainly it does. If anything happens to us nothing will be accomplished anyway."

"Regarding those planets," Mexone said, thinking. "Suppose we *do* want to know what kind of people are going to inhabit them, if any? How can we possibly find out? It will take millions of years for those worlds to cool sufficiently to support life."

"I wouldn't be too sure of that," Abna responded. "Those scientists have created those worlds. If they intend to populate them I can't see them waiting millions of years. You're thinking of the normal processes for cooling: super-scientific power may have a means of cooling them much more rapidly."

The Amazon moved restlessly. "All this is getting us nowhere! We're just standing talking and arriving at no definite decision. We—"

She did not get any further. Suddenly, with the appalling din that seemed to presage activity, 'Old Faithful' burst into life once more. Again the cannon-like explosion; again the mighty jet of steam and boiling water as the geyser blasted forth with infinite power. For exactly the same time as on the previous occasion the outburst lasted...then it quieted again and the disturbance ceased.

"Don't you think we'd better get away from this spot?" Viona asked. "Volcanic seams may open next!"

Abna was staring at the cleft in the rocks from which the geyser had been spouting forth. In the pale twilight from the clouded, newly-created sun his face was thoughtful.

"I wonder if it's possible?" he mused.

"What?" the Amazon demanded, faintly irritated.

"I said a little while back that there ought to be some means of utilizing the vast power of this geyser. Perhaps there is. There's enough force behind it to help project a small spaceship into the void."

"To what purpose?" Viona asked. "Even granting we had a small spaceship, which we obviously haven't."

"We want to find out what the Lords of Creation are driving at, don't we? The only way is to have a close look at those newly-created planets, and hope somehow that they will have been cooled sufficiently to permit of landing on them."

"But this is crazy!" Viona objected. "We've no ship!"

"We have three battered hulks. From those, the rudiments of one small machine might be constructed. What there is missing we'll try and fashion for ourselves."

"Metaphysically?" the Amazon suggested dryly.

"No. By using that..." Abna nodded into the mist wreaths to where a faint, pulsating red from the huge volcanic crater still showed up faintly. "In that crater there will naturally be molten metal. We might be able to make ladles and cast rough moulds to take the metal, depending on what we require. We can fashion long-armed pincers and all kinds of things—make our tools as we go along." He pulled at the nylon thread still attached to the remains of tunic in his hand. "Let's get back to the hulks and see what there is to salvage."

"Just a moment," the Amazon said, restraining him. "All that you have outlined, Abna, might be possible if we had food to sustain us. Without that we'll just go into exhaustion and death."

Abna thought for a moment. His next pronouncement was not particularly consoling to three beings ravenous with hunger.

"Food is just a material means of sustaining a material body. Therefore they're both out of the metaphysical plane."

"Meaning what?" Mexone asked.

"Meaning that this is an occasion where we must rely solely on the force of mind to sustain us. It's perfectly logical because mind always controls the material. I can't possibly handle the situation for all three of you besides myself, so you'll have to help yourselves. Never fear but what you can do it. I repeat—never fear. Once you do, you're lost."

"What do we do?" the Amazon questioned. "As you well know, metaphysics are out of my territory."

"Only because you have never practiced them to any extent. You are well acquainted with the fundamentals of hypnotism and the art of imposing your will on others, and you have a highly trained and sensitive mind. All of you have. This isn't a case of will power: it's the acceptance of the fact that mind, of which you and me and all of us are a part, is an infinite thing which requires no sustenance to keep going at a perfectly energetic level. Think on that ceaselessly; erase for the time being the belief that you have a material body to lug around, and you will surely find you require no food. But remember: never fear! Never for an instant doubt yourself. Right?"

"We can try anyhow," the Amazon said dubiously. "All right—let's get back."

Dwelling on their lesson in metaphysics, the Amazon, Viona., and Mexone followed Abna as he retraced the way across the rocky ground, gradually hauling in his nylon thread as he moved... Inevitably, it brought them back finally to the area of the lurid volcanic crater and the smashed remains of the spaceships. They stood looking at them, each mentally concentrating on the fact that their material bodies did not need food. The Amazon indeed was commencing to believe it as a fact, but for Viona and Mexone the struggle was a severe one.

"The best thing we can do," Abna said, walking amidst the hulks, "is use this machine as the basis of our new space ship. It's the least badly damaged. We need only a fresh nose welding on, and these connections from the engine need reassembling."

The Amazon joined him—then Viona and Mexone. Silently they each, with Abna, went about the task of careful examination and finally arrived at their conclusions.

"One ship in good enough condition to form the groundwork of a bigger one," the Amazon summed up. "The motor's radio controls are irreparably ruined, but we can convert them for manual control. Enough fuel left for one good blast and no more, which will be sufficient to brake us if we want to land on a planet, but not enough for a take-off against gravitational pull, so we'll have to adopt your idea of relying on Old Faithful for the departure. This other ship is so badly damaged that it's useless, but we can use the plates—the sound ones—for adding to our basic ship and doubling its width… That check with your ideas, Abna?"

"Yes, just about," he agreed. "The first job is to get the plates from this other ship and put them in position against this damaged side, then we'll weld them as well as we can with molten metal."

So the task began. Between them, using every vestige of their combined strength, the four hauled the few still sound plates from the smashed-up debris of one of the machines, and placed them in the approximate desired position beside the machine they had chosen, as their intended vessel. This was the heaviest part of the work done, but by no means the easiest. Abna returned to the remains of the machines and began to prod amidst the wreckage in the dim light.

"What now?" the Amazon asked him, leaving Viona and Mexone tackling the job of rewiring the remote controlled motor.

"I want something that will act as a giant spoon or ladle so I can get some molten metal... Ah, this looks promising!"

He pulled forth a four-foot length of flat metal with a broad end. By the time he had finished with it, fashioning it with heavy rock as his hammer, he had an extremely crude, long spoon.

"Splendid!" he exclaimed finally, when the job was done. "This is where I try and descend into that crater—and I don't particularly relish it, either."

"Any help wanted?" the Amazon asked. "Or shall I go and give Viona and Mexone a hand with the radio motor?"

"Better help them. I'll manage this by myself—I hope."

The Amazon hesitated, then: "And when we've done this job, Abna—if we do it—how do we get the ship to the geyser and fix it in position?"

He shrugged. "We carry it between us. What else?"

"You think we're capable of it?"

"All I know is that it's that, or perish. We'll manage it somehow."

Abna turned to go, the ladle in his hand. Then he glanced back and asked a question.

"How are you progressing with the hunger problem?"

"Fairly well. Though I don't guarantee how long I'll be able to keep it up."

Abna said no more; he went on his way towards the glowing, smoking hell of the volcanic crater. He had already seen it once and knew exactly what he was going to find. Even so, as he stood on the precipitous edge overlooking that sea of quivering flame and smoke, he felt profound misgivings. This was going to be no easy job.

It took him nearly half an hour to finally decide on his route of descent—a series of sharp edged rocks which led right down into the heart of the crater, vanishing finally in the red hot hell that was molten metal itself.

Carefully he went down, testing every inch of the way. One slip would have destroyed his balance and plunged him into the flaming morass—but no such thing happened. Inch by inch he went down, heat beating about him in sickening waves, until at last he had reached a position where, shielding himself from the searing heat by means of a rock spur, he could reach out and dip his improvised ladle into the deadly stuff. He withdrew a spoonful and looked at it, gray and shimmering in the uncertain light. Heat began to creep along the handle to his fingers. Immediately he ripped one leg from his shorts with one hand and used its insulation to protect his hand. Then he began to ascend again.

The stuff had cooled to a soft paste by the tine he had reached the ship, and in that condition it was just right for hammering and fashioning into place, sealing up the cracks between the additional plates. The Amazon, Viona and Mexone took on this job between them, using flat bars of metal in lieu of spatulas... Thus, with their line of action established, progress was made fairly rapidly, Abna doing the bulk of the work, and risking the most danger, by means of his constant journeys to and from the volcanic crater.

It was four hours before every crack was welded, and rough tests of the cooled, hardened metal revealed that it was entirely airtight and completely unbreakable except for a violent blow of some kind.

"So far, so good," Abna commented, throwing the ladle away when the job had finished. "Now let's get on with this motor."

Accordingly they all set to work in the now fairly big interior of the vessel to put the motor in order. They stripped it down and removed it, transferring all the radio controls so that the thing could be handled manually. It was crude and anything but reliable, but it was a better bet than staying on this fantastic planet without hope of rescue.

Whether the planet made any sort of revolution or not, they did not know—but certainly there was no sign of night through all the time they worked. Only the clouds, and the dim, heavy diffusion of the newly-created sun. Once its pale rays beamed down and almost immediately vanished again under the smothering clouds.

They slept in shifts—two working and two sleeping, and by this system they gradually accomplished all they set out to do. The climax came when they tested the liquid fuel and its firing potential. Under the manual controls it ignited instantly and jetted a violent outburst of sparks through the rear exhaust fins. Instantly Abna shut off again, profound satisfaction on his face.

"So far we're all right," he said. "Once we're in space natural forces ought to take care of us. The heaviest part of the ship is the loaded rear, with its engine and tail fins. It will therefore offer a greater mass than the rest of the ship and pull us tail-first when we fall into a gravity-field. That's exactly what we want. As we fall we'll blast our rockets down towards the planet we're falling on, and hope that our fall will be cushioned thereby."

"On the other hand," the Amazon said, "what happens if we fall into the gravity-field of that sun? Being the major body it exerts the greatest attraction."

"That's not very likely with us being nearer to the planets than we are to the sun," Abna answered. "They'll pull us first…" He paused and then added seriously, "Let's look this business squarely in the face. We may be going to certain death. We have no means of guiding ourselves: we simply fall into the attraction of whatever planet senses us. The chances are that we'll have enough fuel to escape from one of those small worlds if we want to—and maybe we could head back to the mystery world from which we came. What we do know is that we can never escape from this world under our own power: the gravity is too great. We've got to rely on that geyser for the initial thrust."

"There's nothing we *can* do but gamble," Viona said. "To stop here will finish us. If we have really got to the end, then let's reach it in the endeavor to find something... But if the planet we land on isn't yet cooled, what then?"

"We'll make sure of that while there's still time out in space. If the appearance is molten we'll use what fuel we have to get back to the mystery planet. I know we'll probably be killed when we get there, but we might think of something. While there's life there's hope."

"So," the Amazon said, looking about her in the twilight glow, "there's nothing to do now but transfer this vessel to the geyser and there perch it, fins downward? That it, Abna?"

"That's it."

There was silence for a moment as the four looked at each other. Where Abna and the Amazon looked—and for that matter felt—as strong as ever, Viona and Mexone were obviously not at their best. For all their mental efforts, the claims of hunger were slowly dragging them down.

"I think," Abna said, after a moment, "that it might be as well to go to the geyser site and examine it, and drink at the same time. Come on."

He led the way back across the rocky plain, once

again using his nylon thread device as a guide to the way back. The others followed him without a word, but the Amazon and Abna, who were together, noticed that once or twice during the short journey Viona stumbled from sheer hunger-weariness and would have fallen had not Mexone grabbed at her.

"We've got to find food somehow," Abna muttered. "Those two don't seem capable of practicing the metaphysical side of the problem. Maybe I can try and do it for them for awhile before we start moving the ship."

The Amazon said nothing. She had enough concentration of her own on hand to master her own difficulties. How Abna proposed to handle things for Viona and Mexone as well as keep himself in order was something she could not even imagine.

At the geyser site the pools of water once again provided all that was needed to slake thirst. For a while after this both Viona and Mexone perked up, but by the time the site had been examined for the best position for the spaceship they were once more commencing to droop.

"Let's get back," Abna said, recoiling the nylon thread into his hand. "And while we do it," he added, glancing at Mexone and Viona immediately behind, "I'll try and help your hunger difficulties. Give me all the assistance you can."

What he actually did on the journey back none but he knew, but Viona and Mexone were aware of the fact that the gnawing pains of hunger gradually left them, and their minds became better adapted to realizing the fact that they were indeed masters of their bodies no matter what the apparent fact to the contrary.

"Better now?" Abna asked, when they were back at the crudely fashioned spaceship.

"For the time being, yes," Viona agreed. "I don't know what you did but it certainly worked."

"Good! Concentrate only on your well-being... Now for other things. Between us we've got to lift this spaceship and convey it to the geyser site. It'll be a feat of strength such as we have never had to attempt before. Viona—Mexone, take each side of the center. Vi, take the tail. I'll take the nose."

They moved into position and Abna cast a quick eye over their positions; then he nodded in satisfaction.

"Right... Up we go!"

At his word they all exerted their strength to the full, and as a consequence the mass of the spaceship rose from the rocky ground. It was certainly of considerable heaviness, hut not so much so that it was impossible to move. Granting the strength of the four was approximately that of forty normal people—ten times normal to each one—there was nothing impossible about the job. Like ants, able to move many times their own weight, they struggled mightily along the rocky ground, bearing the ponderous weight on their shoulders and then pausing for a moment and lowering the vessel whilst they recovered from the strain.

Viona and Mexone, deliberately placed in the center by Abna, took the least of the load, which was just as well in their exhausted condition. The Amazon and Abna himself had an equal balance of strain, to which they responded magnificently. They shoved and heaved and lifted, muscles rolling under the effort, and little by little the clumsy mass moved ever nearer to the selected site.

Four times during the trip 'Old Faithful' gushed forth with mighty force, and died just as abruptly— then at last the disheveled, perspiring Abna and the Amazon grinned at each other round opposite ends of the machine as they made the last move to the cleft where the geyser spouted forth. This maneuver was made immediately after one of the eruptions.

"Well, we've got here," Abna said, breathing hard as he joined the other three, "We've roughly half an hour before the next outburst from 'Old Faithful.' In that time we want the tail fins bedded down and the nose at ninety degrees; then we've got to scramble into the control room, close the airlock, and stand by for firing the motor at the identical moment 'Old Faithful' erupts. That way we ought to plunge into space with the minimum of fuel... Now are we ready to heave the nose up?"

"Ready," the Amazon confirmed. "And we'd better watch ourselves in how we do it: if we get off balance for a single moment the whole lot will come crashing down and smash open the plates. They won't stand violent concussion, remember."

"I know," Abna said quietly. "Anyway, we'll do our best. Let's go."

Carefully they worked out their positions. Abna,

Viona, and the Amazon elected to heave the mass upwards, whilst Mexone on the further side was in charge of keeping the balance true and directing the others. Then the struggle began—and in comparison to the earlier effort it was a battle indeed to heave that mass upwards against gravitation.

The Amazon and Abna in particular strained their bodies to breaking point, adopting a series of 'steps' for heaving the nose upwards. First the Amazon, with Viona's help, raised the mass a foot, paused for a second, and transferred the strain to Abna. He took it another foot—then the Amazon again, and so on. Once the fulcrum of balance had been reached the strain disappeared and it was then a matter of careful balancing, with Mexone pushing from one side and the other three from the other until the ship was definitely standing on its tail fins and straddling the narrow blow-hole of the geyser.

"Okay—inside!" Abna ordered. "There may be an eruption at any moment."

None of them wasted any time. They climbed nimbly up the various projections of the ship and through the open airlock at the summit. Once within the control room the far wall became their floor, due to the angle of the vessel, but this was no detriment either to them or the controls. Abna, coming last, closed the airlock and then glanced about him.

"Tough while it lasted, but now we're sitting pretty," he commented. "Hang on to something. Once we start going we'll probably do it with a rush…"

The Amazon, Viona, and Mexone settled themselves as well as they could, holding onto the metal pillars that braced the curving walls. Abna stood by the hastily contrived control switches, his hands ready to give the power to the queer fuel that controlled the rockets.

Moments passed. They began to wonder if, for some reason, 'Old Faithful' was not going to operate—and it was just as they were debating this unpleasant possibility that things began to happen. Through the walls of the vessel they felt a growing vibration, and although no sound reached them through the insulation they guessed that the preliminary rumbles of the geyser had begun.

Within seconds the actual outburst arrived. The window was suddenly clouded in steam and drops of boiling water. Abna closed the power switches and with what must have been an amazing confusion outside the crazy vessel shot upwards, lifted by both its jets and the terrific force of the geyser column.

Air screamed as they shot through it with mounting velocity. Clouds writhed apart. Abna shut off the rockets within a few minutes, having used hardly any of the fuel, but the ship kept on, forced by the pressures of the geyser to the limit of the atmosphere.

They kept going, moving faster than gravity could drag them back. The water on the window froze swiftly as they still climbed. It changed to solid ice as they soared beyond the atmospheric range into the depths of space. They were, for the moment, in a sealed prison, their view limited to the one window where the light of the newborn sun flashed prismatically through the ice crystals.

CHAPTER 4

PLANET OF MONSTROSITIES

Abna snapped the switches that controlled the heaters, then he turned and grinned at the others. They were half on the wall and half on the floor as the vessel was slowly turning onto a more even keel, already under the influence of distant gravitation—probably that of the newly created system.

"Well, we got out of that one anyway," Abna commented, watching the ice on the window slowly commencing to thaw. "What happens next we'll decide when we can see which way we're going."

The four of them waited until the vessel had assumed a more level position, after which movement was not difficult for the ship was traveling fast enough to give a normal gravity, the acceleration being just sufficient for this purpose... Then they moved to the window and peered out of the clear stretches where the ice had melted away.

Ahead of them was that new system of six planets, all circling the small deeply yellow sun. They were pursuing varying orbits at a considerable velocity, though not as fast as had been the case at the outset. Each of the planets was wreathed now in dense cloud, which at least bespoke of an atmosphere, but on the other hand it made observation of the surfaces impossible—and that was a decided drawback.

"Well?" the Amazon questioned. "What do we do, Abna? We don't know what the surfaces are like. To judge from the clouds there's a good deal of heat on each planet. If we land to find molten conditions it'll be the finish."

Abna drummed his fingers in indecision. "We have no telescope, no instruments— Nothing with which to make an assessment of the conditions. No explorers ever worked under greater difficulties. If we crash too hard the ship will fall apart; if we land in molten metal we shan't need to be concerned about events anyway. I just don't know what we ought to do."

"There can't possibly be living beings on any of those planets as yet," Mexone said. "No form of life as we understand it, anyway. Cooling hasn't progressed far enough."

"It doesn't seem so," the Amazon agreed, staring through the now practically cleared window, "and yet—"

She stopped and looked more intently, fixedly, as something attracted her attention.

"What do you make of that?" she asked finally— and for a moment the others did not reply. They had seen the cause of her sudden interest, but they couldn't explain it. Around each of the six planets was a hazy aura, created by a beam—which in turn radiated back-wards into space.

The Amazon moved closer to the window, studying each beam, and it did not come as any particular surprise to her to observe that the planet of the Lords of Creation was the source of the phenomenon. Six beams were projecting from it…six beams to six planets.

"No idea what's going on," Abna commented finally. "In any case there's nothing we can do about it except keep going. If, when we get nearer, we don't like what we see, we'll do our best to escape."

There was silence for a moment, then the Amazon said, "From the look of things this spaceship is likely to cross that nearest beam—the one concentrated on the outside sixth planet—I hope the beam hasn't any disintegrative quality otherwise our number will be up."

Abna considered. "I don't think there's any reason to fear trouble. If there were disintegrative qualities it would be obvious on the planets themselves, and all seems to be well."

This was true enough, but nevertheless all four of them could not help a certain amount of tense expectancy as the crazy little vessel flew onwards, being pulled inevitably towards the gravitation of the outermost planet. They had no idea how long a time elapsed before they finally crossed the beam—but they certainly knew when it did happen.

Fortunately the vessel was traveling at high speed, so the effect of the beam had come and gone almost immediately—but even in that short time the window became a solid glaze of ice despite the warmth inside the machine, and at the same time the none-too-secure plates seemed to sing and vibrate under a high supersonic vibration... Then the trouble had passed, and four puzzled people glanced at each other.

"Plainly vibration," Viona commented, "but what sort of vibration?"

"Pretty obvious," the Amazon answered. "Cold waves are being directed. Cold waves of an intensity beyond anything we have known before. That's shown by the window icing over immediately. Possibly, had we remained long enough in that beam, the ship would have cracked apart as though immersed in liquid air."

"Which proves one thing," Abna commented. "Those planets are being cooled at a terrific speed by scientific means. For that there's a reason—and I'd suggest that the reason is intended life... This grows interesting. Can we hold out until this outermost one is fit to support life?"

"We can try," the Amazon said, "but how will we know when that moment has arrived?"

"All we can do is wait for the beams to be extinguished—at least the one on the outermost planet. That ought to be our signal."

The Amazon looked through the window onto the 'tennis ball' towards which they were moving. She made mental calculations of their speed, and distance from the planet. Then she gave a troubled glance. "At our present velocity—which is bound to increase as we come nearer that gravitational field—we've got about twelve hours before we land. If things aren't suitable by then we're going to have to use our precious fuel to keep us away from landing."

Abna shrugged. "We'll take our chance and see what happens. Right now it would be better if you two slept awhile..." and he looked at Viona and Mexone's haggard faces.

"Slept?" Viona was obviously surprised. "Why?"

"Because sleep is as good as food, and neither of you seem to be doing very well at holding the pangs at bay. If you sleep I can help you because your normal wills will be dormant."

"And you and mother?" Viona questioned.

"We'll get by. We seem to have a better mastery of the conditions than you two."

Neither Viona nor Mexone questioned the wisdom of the suggestion. They simply obeyed it and, sprawling on the floor with their heads pillowed on their arms, they soon fell asleep—the sleep of exhaustion indeed. Abna looked down on them, a mighty figure with his bare chest and arms since his tunic had been sacrificed. He frowned briefly, then glanced at the Amazon.

"I don't like it, Vi," he confessed. "Unless we find some food soon those two are going to become a definite liability. I can only help them so far, and no farther."

The Amazon nodded silent agreement but did not pass any comment. For that matter there was nothing much she could say—and in any case she had no wish to disturb Abna's mental concentrations as he presently set to work to help the two...

And the makeshift vessel still flew on, its nose now definitely turned towards the outermost planet. The Amazon remained by the window, leaning against the wall, more wearied by the space journey than she had ever been in her life before, mainly because she had not the least idea what she was getting into. And there was the added worry of having no means of defense if any were to be suddenly needed.

She calculated that more than half the journey to the planet had been covered when the six mysterious cold-beams suddenly faded. Immediately she alerted and tugged at Abna's arm. He turned, his concentrations on the sleeping two at an end.

"Look," she said. "They've switched them off. Does that mean that cooling is complete, do you think?"

"It's possible." Abna studied the void for a moment or two. "Anyway, we'll risk it. If we guess wrong we'll have to accept the consequences."

Though he had made the response lightly, both he and the Amazon knew that they were taking a long chance. Under the cloudbanks of that world there might be any sort of surface—even a morass of molten metal from which no escape was possible. Nevertheless they made no attempt to turn aside, and with the passing of the hours, as Viona and Mexone still slept on peacefully, the little spaceship began to slowly turn its tail round in space as the heaviest part—the rear—came under the influence of the outermost planet's gravitation. In consequence, observation became more difficult, and distinctly oblique, but it was still sufficient… The Amazon and Abna peered down on bunched-up cloudbanks reflecting the glare of the yellow sun.

"If only those clouds would part for a moment or two!" the Amazon muttered, staring down intently. "At least we'd be able to glimpse the surface below."

"On the other hand," Abna said, "even the cloudbanks can tell us a few things. For one thing, they've hardly moved, and that points to a comparatively calm atmosphere below. We don't know what the atmosphere is composed of, of course, but we'll have to test it the hard way…" He gave a final survey of the looming world. "Time we started to think about recoil," he murmured. "The tail's nearly completely swung round."

He turned to the power plant controls and then stood waiting until the machine was finally completely back-to-front. The moment this happened he blasted the rockets on full power, and almost immediately the downward fall to the planet was checked. Even so the machine was traveling at an uncomfortably high velocity for a safe landing.

In a matter of minutes the cloudbanks were swirling round the window as thick fog. Air screamed round the machine as it shot downward, the retarding rocket fins blazing at full strength as Abna made every effort to check the fall. He and the Amazon were both tensed for an overwhelming shock as the ship hurtled down the final thousands of feet….

Fog abruptly vanished and gave place to daylight.

The Amazon had just time to notice a coast plain with an ocean in the far distance—then the ship landed. The concussion was immense, and yet somehow curiously soggy. The window became spattered with great globules of yellow mud, and for a moment or two the ship lurched and slithered through a quagmire... and then became still.

The Amazon picked herself up from the floor, her head reeling, and looked about her. Abna had not fallen; he was hanging onto the engine switches desperately. Viona and Mexone were awake now, but thrown in a heap in the corner. Overhead the great gaps yawned in the roughly welded plates through which air was hissing with the noise of a burst tire.

"Welcome to the outermost planet," Abna said, rather dryly. "I don't pretend to know how we get away from it with the plates smashed like that."

The Amazon looked at the gaping rent overhead and then said:

"We've obviously got a denser atmosphere inside the ship than we have outside, otherwise the escaping air wouldn't hiss like that... Well, we're not dead anyhow, and I suppose that's one consolation."

Abna, Viona and Mexone joined her at the window. In silence they all stood gazing out on the plain of yellow mud, the lowering clouds, and—very distantly—the glimmering of an ocean.

"Not very cheerful," Abna commented at length. "I don't suppose we—"

"Look!" the Amazon interrupted him. "Look out

there—in the mud! Something's growing."

It was not immediately apparent what she meant, until she indicated the shafts of green poking upwards like knife-blades. Tens of thousands of them sprouting in the vastness, and growing swiftly with every second. Awe-struck at the sight of such growth the four watched, and in perhaps five minutes the thin blades of emerald green had become foot-high bushes, and were still growing swiftly, blotting out the view of the yellow mud altogether.

"Growth somehow accelerated," Abna said finally. "Probably another of those rays at work if we could only see it. One thing is clear: this world has cooled sufficiently to support life, and there it is right before us."

For a moment they were all silent, then suddenly remembering immediate things Abna turned to Vtona and Mexone.

"How do you two feel now?"

Viona shrugged. "Somewhat better—and I suppose it's thanks to you. But you know as well as I do that none of us can go on indefinitely without food—or even water now. If only we could solve our personal problems we'd be in shape for other things."

"Perhaps our problems are going to be solved sooner than we think," the Amazon said, staring through the window. "I've been watching these bushes and I do believe they are about to throw forth some kind of fruit. If it's edible and not poisonous we're well away."

Immediately attention was concentrated on the

bushes, and on nothing else. With anxious eyes the four watched the fantastically rapid growth of out-jutting stems and, at the end of them, the formation of a curious object like a pomegranate. There was a suggestion of a weird flower, which quickly withered, and then came the fruit itself. In clusters of four apiece... And having reached this stage in development the bushes started on a fresh growing spurt, climbing over upwards on themselves.

"We're going outside and try that fruit," Abna decided finally, crossing to the airlock. "If it should prove poisonous I know how to offset its effects, whereas you others don't."

He pulled the airlock door and stood for a moment breathing the atmosphere. It was slightly less dense— as the Amazon had said—than that of any other planet they had encountered, so much so it necessitated very short breaths. Otherwise it was completely harmless.

Satisfied so far, Abna stepped out into the mud— and went to his knees instantly. Be stood stock still, fearing quicksand, but at the present depth he seemed to have reached solidity, so he went on again until he reached the nearest bush. From its swaying, growing branches he picked about a dozen 'pomegranates' and then returned with them to the vessel.

Once in the control room he paused only long enough to wipe the mud from his legs, then he bit deeply into one of the fruits and tasted it experimentally.

"Hmm, not bad. Just like orange."

He went on eating, stopping when he had disposed

of half a fruit. The seeds and pips he tossed outside and to the surprise of the four they sprouted instantly and began to form into knife-blades, then quickly into bushes. Meanwhile, the other bushes were towering now to six or seven feet in height and still growing.

"From the taste of this fruit," Abna said, as he waited for something—if anything—to happen—"it's obviously forced. It has a thin quality, and a good deal of liquid that makes a good drink. But it has no 'body.' From which we can assume that these growths are being forced to maturity far ahead of their normal time."

"Obviously more ray work by the Lords of Creation," the Amazon said; then she frowned to herself. "Just the same, they wouldn't go to all this trouble just to sponsor a sort of glorified fruit farm! There must be more behind it than that. Think of the work they've gone to. Created planets, provided them with an atmosphere and a sun, cooled them and now—this!" She waved a hand through the window to where the muddy plain had now gone completely under growth gone mad. "What do you imagine is the idea behind it?"

Abna shrugged. "Sooner or later we'll probably find out—and I hope it isn't too unpleasantly."

Silence again. A human silence, anyway. Through the open airlock came a creaking and 'squeegeeing' noise as tens of thousands of green fruit plants swayed—not with breeze but with fabulous, exuberant growth.

"This fruit's okay," Abna decided, after a long interval. "I don't feel any ill effects, and I certainly would do by now if there was poison at work…go to it, all of you. There's a whole forest of them."

Viona and Mexone did not need to be told. They grabbed what fruits remained and then sat down by the wall to eat and drink them. Abna gave them a glance and then looked at the Amazon.

"I'll get some more," he said. "Looks as if we're going to need them."

Altogether he took three trips in the slimy ooze outside—but by the time he had finished he had brought enough fruit to last them all a considerable period. After that there began the longest and most satisfying repast the four had ever known. They could feel life and strength surging back to them, and with it a rise in their spirits. Black though the situation was it did not sees nearly so black as it had before.

And by the time the feasting was over and all of them were commencing to feel slightly drowsy with reaction a gloom was falling, swiftly descending into twilight.

"Apparently the planet has a revolution," the Amazon remarked, sitting on the floor with her back against the wall. "We weren't sure…"

Even as she spoke it was night. Deep, absolute night that blotted out everything and left only spectral forms against the wall, faintly suggested by the grayer glow coming from the open airlock.

"Wonder how long night lasts?" Abna murmured.

"Doesn't really signify," the Amazon responded. "There's nothing much we can do while it's here so I suggest you and I sleep and leave Viona and Mexone on guard."

"Fair enough," Viona, agreed. "But what are we supposed to be on guard against? There's nothing alive here surely except the plants?"

"Never can tell." Abna settled himself more comfortably. "Anyway, keep your eyes open, both of you."

Mexone got to his feet and lounged over to the gray circle of the open airlock. Viona joined him and for a while they stood gazing out together over the growths that showed up faintly in the darkness. Apparently, from the sound, they were still growing. Viona smiled to herself as, for a moment, she remembered the old fairy story about Jack and the Beanstalk.

"I still can't understand the objective at which the Lords of Creation, are aiming," Mexone murmured at length. "There must be something more than just this, unless you accept the premise that they're reckoning in thousands of years hence—and somehow that doesn't seem a bit like their methods."

Viona shrugged. "I'm as wise as you are, Mexone— or should I say as ignorant? By and large we just don't seem to be getting anywhere, and as far as escape is concerned this planet is just a prison. We haven't got—"

She broke off abruptly, staring skywards. Just for an instant she had seen—or thought she had seen—a trail of amber light streaking under and then into the clouds. She reflected for a moment that it could have been lightning, but if so it was the wrong color, and electricity on any planet must surely assume the same characteristics?

"What's the matter?" Mexone questioned, as she remained silent, watching the sky.

"I don't quite know." Her voice was quiet and filled with uncertainty. "I thought 1 saw a streak of light flash over the sky. If it wasn't lightning, what was it?"

"Some climatic disturbance probably. What else?"

"This may sound silly, but I was wondering if it— There!" Viona broke off and pointed. "Three of them!"

There was no doubt of it now. From one horizon to the other, streaking far overhead when they reached the zenith, came three golden bands of light which faded away as fast as they were created. The glow vaguely lighted the limitless field of fruit bushes and then was gone. Everything was dark again, yet filled with an inescapable hint of danger.

"Well?" Viona asked abruptly, "What do you make of them?"

"I suppose it's absurd, but I'd say they were space-ship exhausts—machines traveling at a high speed without any noise. Just the same it's impossible. This planet can't even be populated yet, let alone have a race developed enough to produce space ships!"

"On the other hand they could have come from the planet of the Lords of Creation! They could even be looking for us."

Mexone was silent, turning the possibility over in his mind. Finally he asked a question.

"What do we do, then? Wait and see what happens,

or wake your father and mother and tell them about it?"

"No need to wake them yet. There's no danger at the moment. We'll see what—"

Viona broke off again. The three amber bands of light had reappeared. This time they were not created so swiftly. As they came more overhead it was perfectly obvious that they were indeed rocket exhausts from three spots of light against the clouds—spots that could be interpreted as spaceships lit from within... Silent and intent Mexone and Viona gazed up at them—then they gave startled gasps as suddenly blazing white light gushed down on them from extremely powerful searchlights.

"Quick!" Mexone gasped. "Away from the airlock..."

He grabbed Viona and they stumbled inside the control room. Even so, the brilliance of white light remained outside for several seconds, turning the wilderness of swaying fruit bushes to ghostly presences. In that space of time every external detail of the wrecked space machine must have been visible— for visual and photographic purposes. Then the glare died and the intensity of darkness shut down. Mexone peered outside cautiously, but the golden streaks of exhaust had now disappeared.

"I don't like it, Viona," Mexone breathed. "Whoever they are they're on to us. It's more than we can tackle alone."

Viona nodded quickly in the dimness. "I think you're right. Better see what mother and father have to suggest."

In a moment or two she awakened them and quickly explained the circumstances. Abna and the Amazon both studied the now dark, empty sky and then fell to thought for a moment.

"One thing seems pretty clear," the Amazon said at length. "We're under observation, though who by we don't know yet. Like Mexone I can't picture a civilization on this planet. It's only just been created."

"Maybe—but tens of thousands of years have been telescoped," Abna pointed out. "Telescoped by scientific means. If a planet can be cooled so rapidly maybe a civilization has been created as well—somewhere else on the planet, which we were not able to see. And obviously a civilization of high attainments otherwise they wouldn't have space machines..."

He had hardly finished speaking when the three amber trails became visible again. He watched them intently, the Amazon by his side and Viona and Mexone in the background. And this time things seemed to be taking definite shape in that the trails were traveling downwards from the clouds, and coming nearer as they dropped.

"I have the feeling," Abna remarked, "that we are shortly going to come face to face with our unknown friends—or enemies. We have no weapons with which to defend ourselves so if things get tough we'll have to rely further on physical strength or hypnotic power. Probably the former."

The others did not speak. They were watching the

golden trails as finally they came down to ground level and expired at a distance of perhaps a mile away. All was silent once more, and undisturbed. Even the fruit bushes seamed to have ceased their fantastic growing. The dark traceries of their branches thrust out motionless now against the cloudy night sky.

The Amazon asked, "Do we stay in this old wreck until something happens, or do we conceal ourselves outside and see what we're going to be up against?"

"We stay," Abna replied. "Whether we like it or not these unknowns seem to have the power of locating us—so we might as well meet face to face. Standing knee deep in mud outside won't get us anywhere, and if we have to run we'll stand no more chance than flies in molasses."

The decision having been made it was adhered to. In silence the four stood looking out into the night. They were not of course certain that the unknowns would visit them, but it seemed a reasonable possibility—as was presently borne out by events.

It was possibly half an hour after the space machines had landed that there came evidences of activity in the midst of the nearer fruit bushes. And very strange activity it was. In silent amazement the quartet watched what seemed to be firefly-like glows moving in and out of the vegetation. Whether it was the unknowns themselves or the lights they were carrying was not immediately certain—but at length the mysterious glows became clearer and six of them emerged from the vegetation and came to a halt, as though appraising the situation.

"Those—aren't men, surely?" the Amazon demanded, amazed, and for lack of knowing what to say Abna and the others did not answer her. In complete amazement they stared at the outlines of men—the strangest, bizarre outlines imaginable.

Each individual had a totally different shape, and this was distinguishable as a pallid glow, as though the creatures were bathed in phosphorescent paint. But the shapes of them! There were six, but each one was utterly unlike the other. There were bloated bodies and pin sized heads, or vast heads and stick-like bodies. One had hands nearly as big as himself; another had ball-shaped feet and arms that extended to the ground. Yet another had shoulders so wide that he was literally as broad as long.

"Nightmares! Monstrosities!" the Amazon whispered, "We've seen a few queer beings in our travels, but none like this."

"What makes them glow like that?" Viona asked. "They don't need lights to see their way—they're providing their own!"

"Freaks of some kind," Abna muttered. "Or at least they seem so to our way of thinking…"

He would probably have said more but at that moment the beings resumed their advance. Soon they were within a few feet of the airlock and here they stopped again. It was noticeable now that each one had eyes, set in a glowing face. The eyes were various in shape— almond-shaped, very large, very small, and one even had stalked optics which could move individually. A more grotesque and vaguely stomach-turning crowd the Crusaders had never seen.

"We come as friends," Abna said, raising a great arm in the universal sign of peaceful greeting. "Do you understand my language?"

He found the answer to be immediate—in fact all four sensed it at the same time. But it was a telepathic and not an aural reply. Now they came to look carefully the quartet realized that the creatures had no mouths with which to speak anyway. No mouths or noses; only those staring weirdly hypnotic eyes.

"We understand. I speak for all of us," came the answer. "You have no right to be on this planet. The Great Ones—whom you know as the Lords of Creation—our gods and our masters—were under the belief that you perished long ago. It is strange you should still be alive."

"Strange or otherwise, we're here," Abna answered, his words carrying enough thought impact to make sense. "And we seek only to be at peace with you."

"That is impossible. Not only do your thoughts tell us that you hate those whom we revere—our creators—the Lords of Creation; but you are a danger to progress and our plans. What our creators have failed to do we shall complete. We shall destroy you."

"At least they don't mince words—or rather thoughts," the Amazon commented, glancing at Abna. "Apparently they mean it, too. What do we do? Put up a fight?"

Abna shrugged. "I don't think it would do any good. And in any case they're probably catching our thoughts at this very moment—"

"No doubt of it," the Amazon agreed, slowly poising herself for a leap forward, "but you did say that if it came to it we'd have to rely on physical strength or hypnotic power. Well, *my* mind's made up on that score."

With that she acted, with the bewildering speed for which she was remarkable. Whether the six had weapons or not she did not know; but she did know that they had a spaceship, and that was one thing worth having. Her fists were bunched ready for action as she catapulted through the air from the airlock—and in a second or two she landed in the mud within inches of the sextet.

Fantastic heads turned to look at her in surprise, and almost immediately the first blows of her fists landed. Instead of striking hard-packed flesh, however, it was like hitting bags filled with water. The Amazon felt revolted even as she landed her blows, even as thin, cerise-colored blood—if blood it was—splashed on her immediately following a blow.

It struck her as being the most fantastic battle she had ever had. She did not need any assistance! She did not even need the full and terrible power of her muscles. Her flailing fists slashed and plunged into the beings at lightning speed and left them sprawling and dying in the yellow mud through which she herself was floundering. By the time Abna, Mexone and Viona had leapt to help her the six revolting luminous men were sprawled either dead or dying in the morass, their thoughts a chaos of delirium.

"Like a nightmare in reality," the Amazon panted, staring down at them. "Like one of those idiotic dreams you have at times when you struggle with impossible beings..."

"They're easy enough to dispose of, anyhow," Abna said. "Frail, useless bodies housing powerful telepathic minds... What do we do now?"

"Find their spaceship, of course. I know there ought to be three but one will be sufficient. If others of their kind have been left behind we know now how to deal with them. Come on."

She turned actively and squelched through the yellow ooze with its ever-present bushes, which incidentally had indeed ceased to grow. Abna, Viona, and Mexone came up behind her, using the bushes to drag themselves out of the yellow filth. They had only a rough idea where the spaceships had landed and therefore could only proceed in the general direction of where they thought they ought to lie.

"In a way," Abna said, as they sloshed through the mud and near-complete darkness, "it was a pity you made such a wholesale attack on them."

"Why was it? We didn't know what sort of powers they possessed and they made it perfectly clear they were out to destroy us if we didn't act first. I've no regrets, believe me."

"I didn't mean it in that sense. I was just thinking

that if only one of them had been allowed to survive we might have learned a good deal—how there comes to be such intelligent people on this planet, their aims, ambitions, and so forth. That was our main purpose in coming here, wasn't it? To find out what goes on."

"True enough, but I prefer to do it with a reasonable chance of safety—such as we'll have when we take over their spaceship."

"There may be trouble doing that," Viona commented. "There were three ships—and only six people. The rest of the gang will probably be in the ships that have been left behind."

"We'll soon find out anyway," the Amazon said, nodding ahead. "There they are!"

She slowed down her advance for a moment, taking in the scene only a bare fifty yards ahead. The bushes at this point were not quite so dense; not sufficiently so to obscure the view anyhow. There were three small tapering-nosed machines standing in the darkness, their presence signified by a blaze of light through their portholes. One of them—the nearest to the quartet—had its airlock open, the lighted control room vaguely discernable beyond.

"This looks as though it should be easy," the Amazon said. "We should be able to get in and away before the men in the other ships—whom I presume are there—are able to do anything."

With that she moved forward as lithely and swiftly as the mud would allow. Viona, Abna, and Mexone came behind her, alert for the least sign of trouble—

but none seemed to be evident. So they reached the airlock of the machine, which was of considerable size, and quickly moved into the control room.

Then they stopped dead, all four of them on the threshold of the doorway, which led into the control room proper. Four more of the 'monstrosities' were there, protruding eyes turned in expectancy...

CHAPTER 5

BODY SWAP

Only for a second or two did the dead pause last, and in that brief time it was plain that the monstrosities were as astonished as the Crusaders themselves. There came a mixed telepathic communication—that the monstrosities had thought the four were their own comrades returning. On that the Amazon plunged forward, lashing furiously with her fists, sending the queer beings tumbling to the floor helplessly before her iron strength.

"Wait!" Abna shouted desperately, catching at her. "Wait a minute, Vi! Leave them be."

"What!" She swung round, her violet eyes blazing. "Wait for what? While they kill us?"

"There are only four of them. There are also four of us if there's trouble. Leave them alone. Smashing them down is not exactly going to propitiate our name as 'Crusaders,' is it?"

The Amazon relaxed slowly, but her face was grim. She cast a stony glance towards the four creatures as they moved into a corner of the control room and there cowered—literally cowered—in fear of what was coming next.

"My thoughts are reaching you?" Abna demanded of them.

"Your thoughts are reaching us. We plead for only one thing—our lives. We have no orders or wish to harm you."

"For your own sake, that's just as well," Abna responded curtly. "Do exactly as you're told and no harm will come to you. Now, one of you—get that airlock shut!"

One of the beings possessing a head like an over-grown football, obeyed. Then he stood waiting for the next, his protruding eyes full of naked fear.

"Which—if any—of you is the pilot?" Abna questioned; and at that another of the beings, squat and moon-faced came forward.

"Right," Abna said. "Get this vessel into space, and take care none of your fellows in the other machines has any communication from you."

The thoughts went home. Obediently the pilot did as he was told and the machine streaked through the cloudy atmosphere and finally plunged into the void. Only then did Abna give the order to stop accelerating. He relaxed a little and glanced about him.

"Are we likely to be followed?" he questioned.

"Perhaps," came the pilot's thoughts. "But not for some time. It will be assumed that we had separate orders from our creators, which of course we would have to obey."

"Your creators? I assume you mean the Lords of Creation on that distant planet?" Abna nodded to it through the observation window.

"That is so. They are our Masters—the great ones, they who can do no wrong."

"In other words they're the Almighty to these creatures," the Amazon observed cynically, standing by the window with her arms folded.

"Evidently…" Abna considered for a moment. Then, "We do not wish to harm you, my friends, because it's pretty obvious that everything you do against us is forced upon you by your masters. However, our tolerance will only last as long as you do not attack us. You understand that? My thoughts reach you clearly?"

"Quite clearly, Abna of Jupiter," the pilot responded; and from his inclusion of the word 'Jupiter,' Abna's home planet, it was obvious that ha had fully read Abna's mind and history.

"Very well then— We wish to know who you are. Our purpose in life is to crusade against—"

"We know your purpose, Abna. All of it is in your mind. All four of you use your scientific skill to help those planetary races who you think might need it… We do not need it, since our science is probably greater than yours."

Abna said, "Whether you say that because you are being forced to, or whether of your free will I don't know—but—"

"Of our own free will, Abna. Because of the artificial creation of our solar system, the void between our worlds still teems with residual radiation. Given the delicate nature of our bodies it is essential that we guard against it, and so a spaceship is heavily insulated. The commands of our masters cannot reach us through that insulation."

"Which means," the Amazon said, who was also receiving the thoughts, "that we see these beings at the moment as they really are." She considered and then added, "And I certainly don't find them offensive. Quite the contrary."

Abna looked again at the pilot. "There is much that is not clear to us, my friend. My comrades and I saw this world and five others created from a flaming star, which has now become your sun. It is impossible for us to believe that a civilization such as yours can have evolved in so short a time. Can you explain it?"

"Certainly. Have I not said that our science is greater than yours? The worlds were created, yes, and swiftly cooled by scientific means, which I see from your mind you are already aware of. The rest was simply a matter of Time-Control. You understand Time and its relation to space—that too I see from your mind. You can even travel time, to past or future, with machines that you have aboard your own spaceship, the *Ultra*. Am I not right?"

"Quite right," Abna agreed. "At present the *Ultra* is lost somewhere. But continue..."

"The moment the worlds of this newly created system were cooled, other forces took over, forces which enormously accelerated the Time-vibrations existing about any planet in the universe. As a consequence, evolution was accelerated—by several million times, transforming millennia into seconds. Because of that we were born, evolved, and created our enormous science and civilization in a matter of what would be hours to you—standing, as it were, outside the influence of accelerated Time. That condition now no longer exists and things are normal."

"But you would not have time to procreate and bring into being a race," Viona pointed out, puzzled.

The pilot looked at her with his queer eyes. "We do not procreate. Sex is unknown in our species. We are just created, and it is the Lords of Creation who bring this about, That is why we owe them allegiance."

"A race without sex is something unique," the Amazon commented. "You then, and your comrades, are all the original creations?"

"Yes. There will never be any others. And our span of life is practically eternal."

"And all six planets are populated?" Mexone asked.

"Yes, My friend. All six. There are vast civilizations on all of them."

"Which we have never glimpsed," Abna commented, "On this planet all we have seen are multiplying bushes growing at astonishing speed—and nothing more. From a high altitude we surely ought to have seen something else?"

"I think not," the pilot replied, "At that time, when you landed, events were accelerated. You cannot see the individual spokes of a wheel that is turning rapidly, can you? The space between hub and rim appears mistily empty. So it was at the time you landed—an effect that has now ceased. On the fringe of the then existent Time-acceleration were more or less normal conditions, but even there traces of the Time-acceleration existed in the shape of rapidly growing bushes. You will find those bushes are now growing normally—if you ever return to them."

The Amazon mooed forward as Abna stood thinking for a moment or two. After due reflection she asked a rather surprising question.

"Am I correct in thinking that you beings are nuclear in basis?"

There was a brief hesitation as the telepath pilot grappled with the meaning of 'nuclear' then suddenly he seemed to understand.

"Yes, Golden Amazon, we are nuclear, the products of atomic fission. In that way we can be created any time by our masters, who alone have the secret of life from atomic fission."

"Which produces monstrosities of physique, a generally frail body and bone structure, and yet an almost complete immunity to the ravages of disease and natural death since a nuclear creature is constantly radiating enough radioactivity to destroy all the disease germs in existence…" The Amazon nodded slowly to herself. "I thought as much from the moment I saw your weird bodies, your phosphorescent appearance in the dark, and the fact that no two of you resembles his fellow."

"What sort of danger does that put *us* in?" Viona asked uneasily. "We're associating at close quarters with radioactivity!"

"True," the Amazon agreed, "but released in such small amounts by these living beings that I don't think there's any more danger than being near a flash-lamp. They don't emanate as does a radioactive metal; the fact that they have living tissue precludes that possibility…"

"And your purpose in living?" Abna questioned, taking up the questioning again. "What are your aims and ambitions?"

"We live and progress only as our masters decree."

"By compulsion?"

"One might call it that. Mental control over a distance. As children of the Lords of Creation we do as they tell us. They are the masters, magnificent and unquestionable."

Abna said: "Assuming you were alone, undirected—what would your ambition be then?"

"To live as would any other race—and to be happy after our fashion."

"But as it is now? What are your directions?"

"To control the worlds on which we live and then afterwards reach out to other worlds and carry our science to them."

"Conquer them perhaps?"

"If the masters order it that way, yes. As yet we do not know, any of us, what is intended. We merely follow out orders. As I have said, the only place where we are immune from this all-pervading sense of compulsion is inside the insulated regions of a spaceship, such as now."

"I take it," Abna asked, "that you were ordered to come and look for myself and my comrades? It wasn't on your own initiative?"

"Normally we have no initiative. It was directed, yes. We know, as though by instinct, where you were and came to find you. Our intention was to destroy you—but you have so far evaded that intention." The pilot paused and then added, "And as we feel now, with no directions reaching us, you can continue to evade the fate of death which we were intending to mete out to you. Here, we hope you are our friends; once outside the spaceship and our outlook is transformed."

"Strange," the Amazon reflected, "that we also did not sense this mysterious mental compulsion. We were not shielded by any form of insulation."

"You are not natural telepaths," the pilot thought. "Therefore your minds were not affected. Our brains are such that, being made telepathic, they are open receivers to thought, compulsion, and the powers of will, be they for good or for evil."

"All of which," Abna said, crossing to the Amazon, "seems to reveal a good deal. For some reason the Lords of Creation have seen fit to create this fantastic nuclear race, and intend to use them like helpless children to dominate other worlds in time. The idea is not new; we've come up against it many times before, but not in this form. Why go to the trouble of creating six planets and populating them when the Lords of Creation could surely make what conquests they need without any help from anybody?"

"Assuming the Lords of Creation *are* a race," the Amazon pointed out. "We were told that the solitary green light individual whom we met represented the race—one being with all the mental power of his race. Suppose—just suppose—he is not able for some reason to enforce his demands by himself, so has to create races of slaves to do the job for him?"

"An interesting speculation," Abna admitted. "I begin to think that our preoccupation need not be so much with these people and their six planets, as with our friend the Green Light. He has quite a lot of explaining to do if only we can get within talking distance again. Besides that, we want to find out what happened to our *Ultra*, and if it's destroyed find some way to re-create it..."

Viona moved over to them. "Left to themselves these people would be a progressive and practically eternal race. They would only die after thousands of years and all knowledge would be retained in its original state because there would be no handing things on from father to son—or daughter. Since they have no sex and no births that contingency would not arise..." She paused for a moment as imagination took possession of her. "What a unique and brilliant race they would be, if left uncontrolled! Isn't that something worth sponsoring?"

"Certainly it is," Abna agreed, "but there's a lot to

be done before we can pave the way for anything like that. Compulsion has got to cease for one thing, and we want to know the real aims of the Lords of Creation for another. There is no immediate danger of these people extending their power beyond their own system of worlds at the moment, so that gives us time to act." He reflected for a moment and then added positively, "We have got to return to the Green Light, and the Green Light has not got to know he is dealing with us."

"That won't be so easy," the Amazon commented. "The Green Light evidently knew we escaped the coffin ships, and also knew we were on this planet, hence the order to destroy us. How do you propose getting within speaking range without being detected?"

"It requires thought, Vi, but it isn't insoluble. For one thing, it's obvious that these beings look upon the Lords of Creation with a reverence beyond the ordinary. That is what the Green Light expects of them. How then would he react if four of his creations came to his world and stated that they were not so convinced of his omnipotence?"

"His reaction would be...unpredictable," the Amazon said, thinking.

"Even more so if his mental power had no effect on them," Abna proceeded—obviously pursuing some line of thought of his own. "I think there's a way round this—audacious, maybe, but well worth the effort."

"I assume," the Amazon asked, "that the four will be us?"

"Exactly. But we shall look like *them*," and he

nodded to the four radioactive men.

"And how do you propose to create the illusion?"

Abna did not answer immediately. He turned again to the pilot and asked him a question.

"I assume you have knowledge of surgery, my friend—and that it must be of a very advanced nature?"

"Your assumption is correct, Abna of Jupiter. What have you in mind?"

"Could you transfer our brains into your bodies, and leave your own brains and our bodies in cold storage until such time as they would be needed again?"

The pilot reflected briefly, then his thoughts came again. "Yes, Abna—it could be done, but I would warn you of one thing. Once we return to my world we return to compulsion, and even if we could evade it somehow the rest of our race would be under the influence. They would immediately destroy you."

"Taking a long chance, aren't you?" the Amazon demanded. "Don't forget that if we get these bodies we shan't have our normal strength, and that's our one weapon at the moment."

"This is an occasion when we may have to do without it in order to learn something..." Abna's thoughts seemed to be far away; then again he faced the pilot. "Whereabouts are your surgical laboratories?"

"In the center of our city."

"Are they much frequented? Would we be liable to a great deal of interruption?"

"No. The surgical laboratories are only used in the case of accident amongst our numbers, and that happens very seldom."

"And how is surgery performed? You have men specially trained in the art?"

"No. It is entirely automatic. A master-machine is adjusted to make whatever changes are required, and it does it. There is nothing more to it than that."

The Amazon made a rueful face. "I begin to think, Abna, that they were not far wrong in saying their science is greater than ours, even if it is conferred by the Lords of Creation. In medical science they certainly have the mastery."

Abna did not seem to be listening. The plan he had in mind was obviously his sole concern.

"Suppose we could reach this surgery," he continued. "Do I understand that you would set the machine to this required operation and then leave everything to its ministrations?"

"That is so—but the instant we leave this ship we come under compulsion again— so I cannot guarantee what would happen."

"Could we not accomplish our object before the compulsion took hold of you? For instance, supposing we landed within a few yards of the surgical laboratory? Could that be done?"

"Easily. There is a big open space at the rear."

"And how long would it take then to reach this master-machine?"

"About five of your minutes…" The pilot's thoughts stopped for a moment as he considered. Then, "Yes, perhaps it could be done, Abna of Jupiter. We—my fellows and I—have been in space for some time, and the longer we are in it—and shielded by insulation—the longer it takes for orders to impress on our minds again. Certainly it would take more than five of your minutes for us to come under the influence again."

"Good!" Abna exclaimed, his face lightening. "Then that's all we need. Let's get back to your planet right away."

The pilot hesitated for a moment, then, "Though you and your colleagues are masters of the present situation, Abna, you will no longer be so when we get back to our planet. You are willing to gamble with your lives?"

"Yes—because you said you were our friends. I trust to that belief, knowing that whatever else you do is purely the outcome of outside mental influence. You know it is that influence which we are trying to break, to give you and the rest of your race a chance to live in the way you deem best."

"It is for that reason I am willing to help," the pilot said. "I know your thoughts—the thoughts of all of you—and I realize that you are genuine friends. For no other reason would I—or my comrades—have been willing to indulge in your fantastic surgical experiment."

"You admit, then," the Amazon said, "that it is not desirable for you to be controlled throughout your lives by those who made you?"

"Most certainly it is not," the pilot replied. "That is my answer as a free being, insulated by this spaceship. I would have a very different answer were I under compulsion. I see now that you come as liberators of myself, and my race, and as such I shall give every co-operation. If my friends on my own planet and the five neighbor worlds were in my position and free to speak their thoughts, they would take the same decision."

"So be it, then," Abna said, smiling. "And incidentally, since we are going to assume the bodies of yourself and your three friends it might be as well to know your names."

"Of course. I am Vax, and I presume you will take my body. For the others I would suggest Omnas for the Amazon's brain; Kilas for Mexone's; and Jof for Viona's. Our planet, by the way, is known as Xebar."

Abna nodded. "Right! Now we know where we are." He looked at the Amazon, Viona, and Mexone in turn. "Remember the name of the body you're going to have. You'll need it... Now, Vax, we'd better be on our way."

The pilot nodded and turned to his switchboard, adjusting the controls swiftly. In a few moments the machine was slowly turning, then commencing the long, downward plunge to the brightly lighted crescent of a world far below...

* * * *

It was as the vessel finally plunged below the cloudbanks on the sun-risen side of Xebar that the quartet has their first look at the stupendous ruling city of the planet. From the look of it, it might have taken generations of skilled engineers and architects to build it. It seemed incredible that it had been constructed in a matter of moments, thanks to the intervention of accelerated time. From the huge citadels of metal and glass and the thousands of streets radiating in all directions—most of them carrying traffic—the four gained some idea of the high state of society which had been achieved.

Not that they had much time to survey. The spaceship moved so rapidly that they were not permitted much more than a, glimpse, but it was enough to satisfy them that this world of Xebar was no mean planet.

Across the city center with its teeming myriads of beings they flew, until finally they came to a massive building apart from the others, surrounded by sweeping park-like spaces. Obviously the surgical laboratory since Vax headed straight for it, finally bringing the machine down gently perhaps a. hundred yards from the open double doors of the edifice.

"We are ready," he announced, as Abna glanced at him inquiringly. "I only hope that compulsion will not be too strong for me and my fellows when we step into the open... Come."

Opening the airlock he stood for a moment surveying the intervening space between himself and the huge building. Then he looked left and right—obviously to discover if any of his fellows were around. Apparently, however, everywhere within the region of the building was deserted.

"Quick!" came his thoughts. "Follow me!"

With that he left the spaceship and sped away across the square at a surprising speed considering his squat, ridiculous figure. Abna followed after him with giant strides, the Amazon, Viona, and Mexone following in his wake. Behind them again came the other three men of the Xebaric race, looking not unlike carnival balloon effigies as they bobbed, hopped, and jumped across the square.

So up the steps, and into the main entrance hall—a truly enormous place with gleaming immaculate walls and floor. There was no time to look at anything as Vax hurtled onwards. Nor did he stop until he had entered one particular room at the far end of the hall, a surgery from the look of it. Here at last he slowed down, then turned and locked the door behind himself and his fellows. The Crusaders stood waiting, getting their breath back and looking about them.

"So far," came Vax's thoughts, "the powers of compulsion are being easily offset. I do believe we will be able to accomplish the operation successfully. My friends, put yourselves on those tables there, please."

He nodded to a dozen or so long operating tables and led the way across to them; then as the four were about to obey his orders he added,

"Place yourselves on every other table. We four also have to lie down beside you—and the machine will do the rest."

The quartet followed instructions, then from their recumbent positions watched as all but Vax also lay down. He for his part was concerned with an enormous machine on wheels in the center of the surgery, plainly the mechanical surgeon of which he had spoken. He spent nearly five minutes with it, adjusting controls and switches—then evidently satisfied at last he came and lay down on the table beside Abna.

"Everything is in order, my friend," he said. "The brain transference you asked for will commence in a few moments when the delayed action switch operates. You will fell nothing and know nothing, but will awaken in the guise you requested."

"And you, and your comrades?" Abna questioned, his eyes on the machine.

"We shall simply cease to be for as long as you decide to use our bodies. Our brains will be kept alive in a separate surgery—as will your own bodies be preserved. You can see the surgery in question over there. That door with a symbol upon it. You will want to know its location for future reference."

Abna hesitated over saying something, then he thought better of it as the master-machine, with a sudden significant jerk, began to move forward soundlessly over the polished floor. When it reached the tables, and the eight men and women of widely differing worlds, it stopped. Something clicked in its inside and Abna stared in silent wonder into two huge cylindrical lenses that looked like vast eyes. Probably they were replicas of natural eyes, and the gloving radiance that suffused them was plainly of hypnotic basis against which even Abna's immense will was powerless. Not that he really tried to fight the drowsiness that stole over him. He was content to lapse into a soft and soundless darkness...

It seemed only a matter of moments before he was awake again. He opened his eyes to behold the vast machine receding across the floor. In four tall transparent cylinders of cloudy fluid were queer organisms like the inside of a walnut—which to Abna suggested the brains of the four men of Xebar in preserving solution. Whatever they were, the machine was carrying them on one projected arm.

In four other projecting arms lay limp figures—one of them naked to the waist. Abna lay staring at them, recognizing himself, the Amazon, Viona, and Mexone. He still watched, amazed, as the machine drove itself to the symbolized door of the distant anti-surgery, moved a complicated lock with robot fingers, and then passed inside with its load. After an interval it came back, closed the door behind it, and then glided to its former position on the main surgery floor. The whirring within it ceased and it became motionless, its job done.

Abna took a deep breath and fell to looking at, and analyzing himself. He could see now that he had the squat body of Vax, and all the attributes of that radioactive man. Be could sense queer physical differences and something odd about the blood circulation. Otherwise his brain was normal, and his sight and hearing perfect. The only problem came when he tried to open a mouth that was not there.

Sharply he turned and looked at the other tables,

mastering the brief repulsion he felt as he looked at the figures slowly struggling into sitting positions. Mentally he placed them—the one with the head like an outsized football had been Omnas and was now the Amazon herself. The other two, scrawny and pipe-stem limbed, with huge hands and feet, were Viona and Mexone respectively, formerly Kilas and Jof.

Nowhere amongst any of them was there the least sign of an operation having been performed—no scars, no bandages, nothing at all. Slowly the four came to looking at each other, but naturally no words escaped those mouthless faces.

A sudden thought struck Abna—a troublesome, worrying thought. How was communication going to be accomplished? He still had his own brain—all the others had their own—and none of them had the Xebarians' natural gift of being natural telepaths. It was a point that Abna had overlooked, but he certainly remembered it now in all its awful clearness.

Suddenly, almost frantically, he concentrated a question, staring at the being who was the Amazon as he did so.

"Vi, do you sense my thoughts? Do you sense my thoughts?"

After an interval a mental response made itself felt in Abna's mind—weak and indecisive, like a voice heard from a long distance on an indifferent telephone line.

"Yes. I feel what you are trying to convey, Abna."

He hurried on with further concentration. "Our only

means of communication is by thought-transference, but our brains are not normally adapted to the art. Perhaps they can become so. Let us try with Viona and Mexone."

Pause. Then the Amazon nodded her vast head as the communication made itself understandable. But Mexone and Viona, not being in the same highly trained mental range as the Amazon and Abna were completely uncommunicative. They stared in deep wonder... and that was all.

"Leave them be," Abna 'thought.' They will follow us no matter what they do, even if they can't understand or transmit a communication. We ourselves will probably improve with time."

This time the Amazon's response was more rapid. "At least the surgical operation has proven a masterpiece. There is nothing more for us to do here on Xebar, is there?"

"Nothing." Abna slid from the table and stood up, accustoming himself to his strange body. "We are now apparently genuine denizens of this planet—and as such are ready to deal with our mysterious friend the Green Light... And his mental compulsion efforts can't affect us because we haven't that kind of brain. All right, let's be on our way."

"You know where our own bodies are when we need then again?" the Amazon's faraway thoughts questioned.

"Yes. I watched them being taken into that ante-surgery... Now, come, before any difficulties arise." He started towards the door, signaling the silent Mexone and Viona, in their fantastic physical vestment, to follow him.

CHAPTER 6

THE SURVIVOR

The door lock did not prove too much of a problem to Abna's trained mind. He opened it finally and led the way down the enormous hall to the threshold of the main doorway, then he paused and looked cautiously about him. Not that he need have worried. There were none of the nuclear beings in sight. Vax had evidently spoken truth when he had said that the surgical laboratory was used only in case of accident.

The rest was comparatively easy. The four hurried across the square and into the waiting spaceship. Abna closed the door and heaved a sigh of relief from broad, unaccustomed lungs.

"So far, so good," he said, moving to the control board, "It won't take me long to work out how to get this machine moving: I got a pretty good idea of the control system from watching Vax."

And his guess was right. After a few experimental tests he had the machine moving. Swiftly it climbed high above the city—and still higher, until at last the void had been reached.

"One mission accomplished," Abna 'thought' to the Amazon, as he shifted the controls until the fast little vessel was in line to intersect with the orbit of the planet of the Lords of Creation. "Whether the rest will be as easy remains to be seen. I have only one worry—that the Lords of Creation may have seen what we have done. Since they knew our movements when we landed on Xebar, it seems logical to think they must also know about the surgical trick."

"Of that I wouldn't be too sure," the Amazon answered. "It is quite possible that they followed our coffin ships by telescopic means as far as Xebar and gathered that we had escaped the death they had planned—but following us afterwards might not have proved so easy... In any case we've decided what we're going to do, and we're going through with it."

Abna nodded and said no more—or rather thought no more. He wanted a brief spell in which to more thoroughly orientate himself with his new body—and so for that matter did the Amazon, Viona, and Mexone. So each of them, as the space machine flew on swiftly through the void, spent their time exercising their queer bodies and reflecting upon the amazing nature of the experiment that had enabled them to transfer their own brains to these grotesque vestments. Until presently they came against another problem, one that had escaped them as easily as the difficulty of speaking without mouths.

"How do we eat, with faces like this?" Abna asked, and for a long time no thought-reply was evident from the Amazon. When eventually her thoughts came she seemed to have arrived at a considered decision.

"I am not so sure that we need to eat, or even drink. I don't feel either hungry or thirsty. How about you?"

"No," Abna admitted in vague surprise. "I don't."

The Amazon looked at the weird beings who were Viona and Mexone and, by signs, conveyed the same question to then. They shook their heads.

"So there we are," came the Amazon's thoughts. "The matter of food and drink will not worry us. No reason why it should since a body born of, and using, radioactivity would feed on its own energy. Would that human beings were so constructed. It's plain now how almost eternal life is achieved."

Abna did not pursue the subject, mainly because of the difficulties of mental communication. Instead of trying to converse, he, the Amazon, Viona, and Mexone watched the world of the Lords of Creation coming ever nearer, still surrounded by its magnetic varicolored stars. It was a strange thing, but when approached from this side it was perfectly visible as a planet; yet when approach was made from its opposite side—as had been the case at the outset—it appeared only as darkness. Why this was so the four did not attempt to understand. Probably a matter of light-wave deflection since the planet was enigmatic in many respects.

"We may perhaps have a clue as to whether the Green Light has tumbled to our little game in how we arrive," came Abna's thoughts, after a long interval. "When we came in the *Ultra* it was mysteriously stolen from us and we found ourselves on the planet without having any idea how we'd got there. If the same thing happens again we can take it that the Green Light has been watching us."

"True enough," the Amazon agreed. "Whether we have been observed or not, my main wish is to be revenged on that glorified Roman Candle for the way he treated Viona. I haven't forgotten one bit of what he did, and I want recompense."

Abna glanced at her. "Maybe you do, and your sentiments are also mine—but don't jeopardize the safety of all of us just to exact revenge. We have a plan, remember—to find out what the Green Light is driving at and if possible to break the hold he has over the planets and people he has created."

The Amazon did not reply. When it came to exact payment for a wrong she and Abna were always at variance. Where she always struck the moment she had a chance, Abna preferred caution—sometimes to the benefit of all four of them…

So the hours passed and the machine flew on silently at a steady velocity. It was quite a swift, neat vessel even if it did not employ the huge resources or area of the vanished *Ultra*. The planet of the Lords of Creation filled all space now, edged with its magnetic compass points of sapphire, gold, emerald, and ruby light.

"So far we don't seem to have been observed," Abna commented, staring down on the crazy patch-work of the planet's surface. "It's time I slowed us down. Where we land I can't be sure, but if we look for a building with a multitude of steps maybe—" He stopped, glancing about him sharply. Something was happening, something reminiscent of the weird events that had preceded the disappearance of the *Ultra*. The walls were becoming transparent, giving a clear view of the clouds and void beyond them.

"Either we've been observed," came the thoughts of the Amazon, "or else this is the Green Light's normal way of welcoming all visitors. Whatever it is we've no defence against it."

Abna did not reply. He was experiencing the weird sensations of that other occasion—the strange conviction of unreality, as though it were all a vivid waking dream. And even as he, like the others, tried to analyze himself the peculiar conditions resolved themselves. The spaceship faded from view and the four were standing, not in space, but on a polished floor. All around them machines encroached—incredibly complex, and a few feet ahead of them stood a tall tower, a hundred feet high and topped with a mesmeric winking green light. At the base of it was a four-sided enclosure.

"We're back where we started," came the Amazon's laconic thoughts. "The old Green Light himself."

Abna made no response. Though, as far as he knew from previous experience, the Green Light was unable to read thoughts, he did not wish to take the chance of giving himself away... Then he glanced upwards sharply as the emerald glow jerked sharply at a series of words—cold, inquiring words.

"And what is the meaning of this? Why do you leave your planet of Xebar to seek audience with me?"

Abna gave the Amazon a glance. He thought out a comment swiftly.

"He can't read thoughts evidently, otherwise that remark of yours a moment ago would have told him who we are."

"If he had been able to read thoughts," came the Amazon's reply, "he would have had no need to persuade Viona to get the secret of the Zero-Thought Amplifier from us. He would have read it from our minds."

Abna made no response to this. It surprised him that he had neglected to think of this aspect.

"Why do you not answer me?" the Green Light demanded. "You can do by thought waves even if you cannot speak. Answer! Why do you seek an audience with me?"

Abna and the Amazon both hesitated, unsure of their ground again. The Green Light had just said that he could understand communication by thought waves— yet how could this be so if he could not read thoughts?

"The whole thing's trickery," came the Amazon's thoughts, suddenly. "Even as I said at first, he creates an illusion of far-reaching power, but I'll wager most of it is done by mechanical aids. Somehow, Abna, we've got to get to the bottom of this..." Abruptly she turned and faced the Green Light directly. Her words as thoughts, registered clearly in Abna's brain.

"We come for one purpose only—to see face to

face the being who has created us, and to state certain demands."

The Amazon could not be sure but she thought she heard a voice speaking somewhere, a curiously disembodied voice speaking exactly the words she had 'thought.' She frowned to herself over the puzzle; then the sharp-edged voice of the Green Light answered her.

"To make certain demands you say! What right have you to demand anything? I am the master, and I alone."

"As such," Abna 'thought', before the Amazon could reply, "you have no right to maintain your control over us once you have created us. Or at least you ought to explain your reason for the control. What is the object in creating six planets and a nuclear race? What do you require us for?"

Again that disembodied voice, repeating this time Abna's own thoughts, the audible words following a split second behind the thought. Abna was so intent on his communication he probably did not hear this faint echo of his words—but the Amazon did and quietly looked around her for an explanation.

"It is not my purpose," the Green Light responded, "to reveal to you the nature of my plans. You were created as slaves and slaves you shall remain. You have great temerity in suggesting that you should be freed from my control."

"There are ways in which we can enforce it," Abna thought, and once again came the echo. Then before he could proceed any further the Amazon suddenly acted.

Seizing her chance, and realizing the Green Light

was entirely concentrated on Abna, she suddenly leapt forward towards the four-walled enclosure at the base of the Green Light tower. As she moved she flung herself upwards in a flying leap, forgetting for the moment she was not in possession of her own, perfectly attuned body. Normally, she would have easily gained a hand-hold on the top of the enclosing wall. As it was she fell short, her ridiculously sensitive body badly bruised.

"You behave foolishly, friend," the Green Light commented, seeing her useless effort, and with that strange forces gripped her, raised her, and then flung her a dozen feet away. She dropped half stunned to the floor, more bruises and contusions added to her aching body.

"Abna..." Her thoughts reached him as he stared in amazement. "Abna—we must get behind that enclosure! We'll find the answer to everything there!"

He was about to reply to her when there came another unexpected development. Mexone and Viona, standing quietly to one side, had obviously seen the Amazon's abortive effort to scale the wall; and maybe they had also heard the puzzling ghost voice. Whatever it was they abruptly acted together, Mexone flinging himself in a stooped position to the bottom of the walls and Viona leaping onto his back. With her absurdly long body it was an easy job for her to reach the top of the wall... She gained it, stood erect, then leapt forward into space beyond the enclosure, the whole action so swift there was hardly time to grasp what was happening... Even the Green Light did not seem to realize what was intended for he did not make any effort to stop this unexpected intrusion beyond the wall.

With Viona's disappearance beyond the wall Abna woke to action and helped the Amazon up. They hurried forward, behind Mexone who was in the midst of scaling the wall. And throughout it all the Green Light remained as a steady emerald glow and no commanding voice came forth.

"Something's happening," came Abna's thoughts, as he lifted the Amazon to a handhold on the wall. "I don't know what— Right? Have you got a grip?"

The Amazon did not answer. Inwardly cursing the frail muscles of the body she occupied she drew herself to the wall summit and then sat on it, staring beyond. Abna came up beside her, and he too gazed in amazement.

And not without reason! The enclosure beyond was perhaps twelve feet square and dominated by a huge electronic instrument with a keyboard like that of a highly complicated organ. There were 'stops' by the thousand and all manner of buttons—whilst against the walls themselves were screens, radio speakers— banks of unexplainable scientific devices, and a huge compass-like object that linked up by cables to the green light above. Most noticeable of all was a microphone standing to the front of the 'organ manual.'

This much Abna and the Amazon took in at a glance; then they transferred their attention to Viona and Mexone. Between them, using all the strength of their frail bodies, they were holding a man—at least he looked like a man—down in his chair, the chair being positioned so as to face the 'organ' manual. He was struggling fiercely to free himself from the grip of the two, but so far he had not succeeded.

"A man, here? Beyond the Milky Way?" The thoughts of the Amazon registered clearly in Abna's mind.

"That's the way it looks! We'd better investigate."

In a moment or two they had both descended from the wall and moved forward. With their strength added to that of Viona and Mexone the man in the chair did not stand a chance. He sat and glared, with big amber-tinted eyes, which at least showed that his origin was not Earthly, even if his physique was on the same lines. He made another fierce effort to tear free of the grip upon him, and it was in that moment that the Amazon noticed something. He had no legs! Either this was a natural oddity of physique or else he had had them amputated. Whatever the real answer, his body ended at his waist.

"All right," he said bitterly. "You win, my friends! Let me go. I've no facilities for harming you, whilst you're in here. Only when you're outside."

It was noticeable that his voice was similar to that of the Green Light, only now there was no harsh, mechanical intermediary in the form of a microphone.

"I know who you are," he added dryly. "I spoke in English when you first arrived, and you answered me immediately—even if it was by thought. That made it you couldn't be anybody else but the Crusaders since the people of Xebar haven't been trained to understand English. If they communicated with you, it was because your thoughts resolved into their own language, which made sense."

The Amazon gave Abna, a grim look. Her thoughts made an observation.

"Evidently we went through a great deal of effort for no real purpose. Our friend here saw through the trick. It never occurred to me that language should give us away."

Abna shrugged. "Nor to me. It seems that we overlooked quite a few things. Not that it matters since we've accomplished our purpose in the end and got our friend where we want him."

The Amazon 'said': "Go beyond the enclosure again, Abna, and 'think' a worded communication. I want to satisfy myself on something."

Though he looked puzzled Abna obeyed the behest. He quickly climbed the wall to the exterior hall again, and the Amazon, Viona, and Mexone glanced towards a screen as Abna—in Vax's body of course—became visible on one of the countless visi-plates. Then, reedily, as his thoughts formed a sentence, a voice spoke in a nearby speaker. A quiet, hardly audible voice, but loud enough for anybody with normal hearing to pick it up.

"This is Abna speaking. I don't know why I am doing this, but I have been asked to do so."

With that he moved from the screen and reappeared over the wall. He jumped down into the enclosure and came to the Amazon's side.

"Well?" asked his thoughts. "Are you satisfied?"

"In that respect, yes. When you directly concentrate your thoughts into a spoken sentence, and providing you are squarely facing this way, invisible devices pick your thoughts up and convert them into normal speech, which I presume is a modification of the principle of transforming light-impressions into sound as is done on a film soundtrack. Because your thoughts were expressed in the English language, the English language came forth—and incidentally gave us away. I heard the echo of your thought-sentences in here, which evidently came from this low-power speaker."

"Mmm, all very intriguing but not particularly explicit." Abna turned to the man in the chair and gripped him fiercely. "What's the explanation of all this? Who are you and what are you driving at?"

"You're wasting your time," the Amazon said. "He can't read your thoughts, remember."

"I'd forgotten... But there must be some way to get the answer to all this mumbo-jumbo."

"Certainly there is—I'll go outside and mentally concentrate on questions, which will assume audible speech in here. Our friend here will reply in the ordinary way as the Green Light. Keep a close watch on him, too."

With that the Amazon turned, climbed over the wall, and went into the hall beyond. In the enclosure, Abna, Viona, and Mexone watched her appear presently in the visi-screen. The man in the chair watched too, his powerful mouth clamped shut in a manner that indicated he intended to be stubborn.

"Now, my friend," came the gentle interpreted voice from the loudspeaker, "There's a good deal to clear up, and you are the only one who can do it. Firstly, who are you, and what is your purpose in being here?"

The man hesitated through a long interval, then Abna gripped his arm and pressed hard on the bone. Though in the guise of Vax his strength was not very great, he nevertheless used a special hold which, if necessary, could bring a good deal of pain to the man in the chair.

"Answer!" the Amazon snapped. "You gave us little chance when we were at your mercy. Do not expect us to give any in return."

"My name is Und," the man said at last. "I am an outcast of the planet Calion. Indeed not so much an outcast as the last survivor of my race, which had earlier originated on another planet."

"And where was that other planet?" the Amazon questioned.

"Our home world is the fourth planet from a star you call Procyon."

"Procyon," the Amazon repeated slowly. "A star just over 11 light years from Earth."

"That is so," Und agreed. Our name for my world is Valdon."

The Amazon gave a start as a suspicion began to slowly unfold in her mind, prompted by the fact that Procyon was—cosmically speaking—very near to Earth. She was recalling the events of the time not long before she had met Abna. "You assert that you left

Calion and traveled alone through interstellar space? How is that possible when it would take you countless lifetimes to make the journey?"

"You made the journey yourselves, did you not?"

"True, but in a machine capable of circumventing the law of Fitzgerald's Contraction by rotating into hyperspace."

"You are not alone in that scientific achievement, Golden Amazon. The only difference in my case is that I landed badly, which resulted in the loss of my legs, and no matter how efficient artificial legs can be they are not—and never can be—the equal of the originals. And for technical and biological reasons it is impossible for me to graft new limbs onto the old stumps..."

Und paused for a moment as though collecting his thoughts. Then he went on again.

"At first sight it may seem strange that we—all of the same region of the Galaxy—should meet here in the Milky Way Galaxy. But actually, possessing similar scientific ways of winging space, it is not so remarkable. I have, as I told you earlier, kept a constant observation of your activities and I still believe you are a menace to scientific progress."

"Only because you have the wrong idea of our purpose," the Amazon retorted. "Answer me this! Why did you leave Valdon—or Calion—and come here?"

"My race left Valdon when our planet was afflicted by the *ursurgas*, infinitesimal life-forms born of iron. Iron is the basic material of all solar system, common to every planet, and the *ursurgas* exist in every particle of iron—but they cannot breed or come to life without a certain radiation of a sun chemically exciting them. The radiation is known in your science as the seventh octave, and it is shielded from you by your atmospheric blanket, which is why your iron was perfectly safe. When our surface atmosphere thinned, the seventh octave got through and bred this iron-eating life in every particle of iron, bringing our civilization to its knees. In the end, in an incredibly short space of time, it reduced the surface of Valdon to a waste of ferrous oxide.

"We found a way to kill them, but it came too late to save our surface life being destroyed. We decided that interstellar migration was the only way to save our race. We formed a space armada, which we split into two groups, heading in opposite directions to increase our chances of finding a new home. One armada headed for—"

"That I already know," the Amazon stated. "One half of your race attempted the invasion of Earth—but were defeated by me. More than that—I wiped them out utterly by tricking their entire fleet of space-ships into following my own ship too near to the sun. They got caught in his massive gravity field and were consumed." The Amazon smiled grimly as Und glared his hatred.

"So you deliberately destroyed the remnants of my race on Valdon by hurling them into the sun?"

"I do not regret it. They deserved death. They got it. However, I did not know that there were any survivors of that alien race."

"There probably weren't, but *my* companions were not part of that invasion fleet," Und snapped. "I said that only *half* of my race moved to your solar system. The other half migrated into space in another direction, seeking new worlds on which to settle and continue our race, using spaceships equipped for hyperspace travel to circumvent the limiting speed of light.

"Eventually we found a planet, Calion, capable of supporting our type of life, and we colonized it. We began to rebuild our civilization, until, in the course of experiments into biological surgery a virus was unwittingly created, and released. It was deadly in the extreme. Not only did it consume living beings like wildfire, but also vegetation. In the end, in an incredibly short space of time, it reduced our new civilization to ruin... naturally, seeing what was coming, many of us made efforts to again escape into space. I was one of the many. Other machines—spaceships—once again flew to different parts of the universe to try and rehabilitate themselves and as far as I am concerned, were never heard of again. In my own spaceship the original crew of twelve skilled scientists finished with only one... myself. The others died from traces of the virus we had unwittingly carried with us and I was alone in space, without company and without a world."

"How was it that you alone survived?" the Amazon queried.

Und shrugged. "It was a biological fluke. My immune system was able to counteract the virus, to almost destroy it—"

"Almost?" the Amazon asked, puzzled.

"It is still dormant within me," Und explained, his voice bitter. "That is why I cannot graft new limbs onto my body. They would not possess my own immunity and the dormant virus would revive and destroy them. The same thing would happen if I transplanted my brain into another body—as you have done."

"And how did you come to be on this world?" the Amazon questioned.

"Ultimately, after covering vast distances in space, I saw this planet. Telescopically it showed itself as a machine world covered with negative light—which, interpreted, means darkness. There were apparently no inhabitants, and yet a wealth of scientific instruments. It seemed a reasonable gamble, so I descended on it. In the darkness I misjudged my distance and landed violently, smashing up my vessel...

"That very action of landing must have done something. It released some kind of automatic process and this whole fantastic planet came to life. Mechanical beings came to rescue me. These same mechanical beings performed amputation and restored me to comparative health. These same mechanical beings gave me food, shelter, and all the information I needed..." Und paused and then added slowly, "But they *were* only mechanical. I soon grasped that fact. I soon also grasped that this planet was actually a vast scientific heritage, the original creators of it long since vanished, but they had left behind them a world which could—and did—

come to life the moment a visitor came within range of the invisible beams always projecting into space."

"You mean that the whole planet was normally inert and all the machinery inoperative except for invisible beams projecting into space?" the Amazon asked. "When you crossed the beams in your spaceship they reacted—like a selenium cell unit can open a door when a person crosses its invisible rays?"

"Exactly... After a short while I realized that some unknown race had handed me a world of vast resources on a golden plate. There was nothing this planet could not do with its range of scientific instruments, all of them far ahead of even my own science. I set myself to work to discover what limitations there were, and I found quite a few. For one thing, despite the almost superlative surgical mechanics which exist here, I could not have new legs, chiefly because of the accursed virus within my body... That was to be my biggest handicap—a world of infinite resources at my command, a mastery of time, space, and the mental arts—yet here was I completely limited because of my ruined body. What then, was my best course?"

"Create living beings to work for you?" the Amazon suggested grimly.

"Correct, living beings, far more efficient that even the cleverest robot, provided—always provided—they are mentally controlled. My reasoning was this: my main desire is to restore the lost glory of my world of Valdon, bring the planet up once again to the zenith of scientific power it possessed before the *ursurgas* plague. That danger will now have passed away and reconstruction can begin... So, with the devices here at my command I created a sun and six planets, and then from nuclear fission basis populated those worlds with beings who are to become the new Valdonian race. I performed miracles of science from this master control board here. I cooled the planets, accelerated Time itself—made my nuclear children telepaths— which gives them an enormous advantage—and also made them incapable of hunger and thirst. A virtually eternal race. Six worlds full of them, and all mine. All of them ready to obey me because they can do no other."

"You admit, then," the Amazon asked, "that most of the 'effects' produced on this planet are not purely mind force—as you suggested—but actually scientific illusions and electronic magic?"

"Yes, I admit that now," Und responded. "I am not the pooled information of a race, as I said at first. That was merely bluff. I have told you exactly what my aims are—the rehabilitation of Valdon in due time."

"Rehabilitation by nuclear beings?" the Amazon asked. "Weak, fragile creatures with controlled brains. Delicate, no matter how great their other attainments. One bomb could destroy them in their tens of thousands, Und."

"You talk violently, Amazon, as usual. Not constructively. Naturally they would work out how to defend themselves against any bomb, possibly using force screens. They can, and will, restore the lost glory of

Valdon, and I shall be at their head, which is right as the only surviving member of my race."

"There may be others. You said many ships left Valdon originally, and later Calion. That you haven't seen anything of them since does not say they no longer exist."

"If they do, they will ultimately come back to restore Valdon—to do as I say. I shall be indisputable—the master. Don't you see, Amazon? I had no other means of restoring my planet. I could not force the beings of some other world to desert their own planet and rehabilitate mine. I needed an original race of people dedicated solely to the restoration of Valdon. I could not begin a race myself due to their being no females, and again there was the time problem."

"I suppose cloning yourself was impossible because of the virus permeating your entire cellular structure?" the Amazon asked.

"Yes. The only answer was to create a race, sexless, telepathic, and eternal. They are the Valdonian people of the future. When they have restored my world they shall go back to it."

"You needed six planets full of people to rehabilitate only one world?" the Amazon asked in surprise.

"Five of the planets in the six-system which I created will remain untouched for the time being. Only the inhabitants of Xebar will be used to start with, to lay the foundations of the new Valdon."

"And then?" Cold disbelief crept into the Amazon's thoughts and voice. "You're not fooling me, Und. What you intend is first the restoration of your world, and after that the colonization of the other worlds in the Earth system. You intend to make your home planet the jumping off place for an eventual conquest of the Earth—to get your revenge for my wiping out your earlier invasion fleet!"

"If you wish to think that I cannot prevent you having your dreams," Und responded evasively.

"It is not a case of thinking it, Und, it is an obvious fact. There are no worlds in this sector of the Galaxy that you consider worth your while to dominate. The risk to you would be too great. They might even have science of such a high order that it would destroy you instantly; but with the Earth solar system you're on safe ground because Earth does not contain life sufficiently advanced to oppose your nuclear race with its refined science. Eventual domination of the Solar System is your objective, and this incredible scientific planet is your stepping stone."

"As you wish," Und shrugged. "I can see that once again you are trying to find grounds to interfere, which is one reason why I have already tried to destroy you, so far without success. You may be interested to know that powerful telescopic devices watched you land on Xebar, and I again endeavored to be rid of you by issuing mental orders to my nuclear slaves. Unfortunately you still live...at the moment. It has always been easy to follow your movements, so complete is this planet in scientific apparatus, I could watch and speak to you, over hundreds of miles, as when you first landed here. I could move you bodily from place to place as required, all by invisible rays. You have no idea how intricate and how satisfying this planet can be."

"And yet you sit in your chair held down by three of your own creations using the brains of Abna, Viona, and Mexone," the Amazon responded dryly. "Your mighty powers are not so perfect, perhaps?"

"Just a miscalculation," came the cold response. "I often thought I should have this enclosure roofed in. I would have been able to save myself had that been done."

"Why is there no roof?" the Amazon asked, genuinely puzzled.

"I have no idea. There has never been one. Nor are there any anywhere on the planet. I can only assume that the original scientists of this planet were two-dimensional—worm-like—and therefore to such as them a roof would have no meaning. On the other hand," Und continued, "the absence of roof is useful. It enables me to see if the green light is operating correctly in response to my words. I could see it by mirror reflection or closed circuits I know, but they have their disadvantages. That green light is the eye of this whole vast scientific assembly, Amazon. From it is directed nearly everything in the matter of thought wave, words, control of movements… even the waves of compulsion which reach out to Xebar and the neighboring planets…"

Silence—for a long time. Then the Amazon made one of her dry comments.

"It is surprisingly useful, Und, that you understand the English language, otherwise our long communication would not have been of much use."

"English was known long to all my race when Valdon had its civilization. Not only English, but other Earth languages as well. It is strange that the Earth peoples don't adopt one language for all their people."

Suddenly Und acted! It was abrupt, coming right at the end of his sentence when Abna, Viona, and Mexone were not expecting it. In any case they had been so interested in listening they had almost forgotten their vigilance—as they found now to their cost.

In a few seconds Und lunged forward in his chair with his legless body, his arms lashing sideways to send the delicate Abna, Viona, and Mexone reeling backwards. The instant he was free Und jammed his broad hands on the huge manual in front of him, and in those lightning moments he achieved victory.

Tubes flared; nameless forces operated. The quartet in the borrowed bodies of the Xebarians realized they were paralyzed, could not as much as move one foot before the other…

CHAPTER 7

ALL-IN-ONE

Und relaxed slowly in his chair and then turned his face towards Abna, Viona, and Mexone as they crouched, perforce immovable, a few feet away from him. He smiled slowly—a peculiarly hideous smile that split his square, unsentimental face from ear to ear. Now they came to look at him directly the three Crusaders realized what a harsh intellectual this descendant of faraway Valdon really was, an effect heightened by the amber tinted eye-irises and upwardly sweeping forehead, which terminated in total baldness. Unquestionably a being to be wary of, even more so with such a mass of scientific equipment around him.

"I find this most satisfactory," he said presently, glancing at the immovable Amazon reflected in the visi-screen. "All four of you back again in the position where you were at first—completely at my mercy for all your efforts at body exchange and so forth. And incidentally," he went on, his voice calm with the assurance of victory, "I was not bluffing in our earlier encounter when I said I had watched your various exploits from afar. I spoke truth—and nothing you have done has convinced me that you should continue to crusade, even less so since you, Amazon, have formed the theory that I and the race I have made constitute a threat to the Earthly solar system."

The Amazon's body was paralyzed but not her thoughts. They came through the loudspeaker as before.

"That was not a theory, Und. It was a statement of fact. You and your race, now we know the facts, constitute one of the biggest threats to peace and progress that has ever been known."

Und shrugged. "Very well, I admit that. In the end it will be Valdon only that matters—Valdon and Und. The rest of the planets will merely be subservient… But that is in a future which you will never see." He mused for a moment then added, "I have just been deciding what I ought to do with you. Death is the obvious answer, but you might somehow evade it—and besides it is a trifle too swift after the trouble you've caused me. I think it might be poetic if all of you helped in the colonization of Valdon, don't you think? Forced to do it against your will. First on Xebar, arranging the preliminary details, then on Valdon itself."

There was a long silence, then Und resumed, "Yes, poetic indeed—but something more must be added. One moment."

He operated several keys on the manual and then considered the result on displays above his head. Finally he made a comment.

"Apparently your brains are such that they are not affected by the compulsion waves which I direct at Xebar and the neighboring worlds. That must be because you are not *natural* telepaths with highly receptive brain-centers, although you have some rudimentary ability. Very well—the condition shall be corrected to *make* you telepaths, then you will be completely under my control. Also..." Und meditated for a moment. "Also, my friends, there is a finishing touch which I think will prove unique. One might consider it a form of punishment. In, any case it will be effective... I shall merge all four of you into one."

"You'll what?" the Amazon asked in amazement.

"Merge all of you into one person. Four brains—converted to telepathic control—and four bodies, all in one. The characteristics of each of you embodied in the one unit. That will mean that the four beings of Xebar who have given you their bodies will never regain them. It will also mean that each one of you is under the dictates of the other. Never again will you act individually. Never again can you spring separate surprises. You must always move as one, and you will always be under the mental compulsion of myself. Exquisite! That should be the end of the Cosmic Crusaders for all time..."

"Why is it that a man of your far reaching intelligence does not try to be magnanimous for once?" the Amazon demanded. "Why all this effort to restore lost glories, to condemn us to mental and physical incarceration, to control the races of six worlds who desire only to live and progress naturally? Who are you to take on the mantle of the Almighty and decide what shall be done? Nothing can come of it—*nothing!*"

Und gave his broad smile. "Naturally you fear for what is coming, Amazon—and I cannot say that I blame you. Otherwise you would not be moved to such impassioned thoughts!"

"As yet," came the Amazon's thoughts, "you can obviously see no error in your plans. You have a scientific planet behind you, your enemies at your mercy, and the races of six worlds created specially to do your bidding. Yet with all this, it would be safer for you if you destroyed the six worlds and their peoples with the Zero-Thought Amplifier, and let us go free. I don't pretend to read the future, but sometimes I get glimpses of what is to come, and your own fate will not be a pleasant one if you persist in this scheme of rehabilitation."

"Excellent phrases, Amazon, but not of the least interest. I am decided what I shall do—and I shall do it. As for the Zero-Thought Amplifier, the plan of which you gave me—"

"To prevent further suffering on the part of Viona!"

"As for the Amplifier," Und proceeded, "I shall use it—or at least make it—when I consider the time ripe."

The Amazon's thoughts came again, this time with a slight change of mood.

"Didn't you forget yourself for a moment just there, Und? You said you'd 'use' the Amplifier, then quickly changed it to 'make it.' I suspect, as I did before, that neither the *Ultra* nor the Amplifier have been destroyed. It's all part of the science of this planet—the science of hallucination, probably incorporating the fourth dimension."

"I am not disposed to argue over the matter," Und retorted, but it was obvious from his manner than he had been caught out. "It is time for action—not words. So I'll bid you farewell, my friends, with my congratulations on a splendid but quite useless effort!"

He turned to the manual again, operating all manner of keys with the skill of a professional typist. In consequence strange things happened as the multiform scientific gadgets of the strange planet went into action.

First, Abna, Viona, and Mexone found the paralysis was receding from then, but even so they were not capable of any violent action since other powers came almost instantly into action. They were swung by invisible hands and forced to the wall of the enclosure where a door suddenly opened—much to their surprise. Thence they were forced to cross the machine-room floor until they had reached the side of the Amazon. She was still in the grip of the paralysis, but it relaxed as the other three gained her side. But as it was for them, so for her: she was incapable of action. All she could do was helplessly go where the invisible guiding powers pushed her...

Unable to help themselves the four were relentlessly shoved to a remote region of the machine room, ending their journey in what was plainly some kind of immensely complicated medical surgery. Even as they studied incomprehensible machines they were lifted bodily and placed on long bunks, or rather shelves, one above the other. Machines began to move towards them on noiseless wheels. Weird instruments glittered in the curious ruby lighting… Then the four were no longer conscious as an odorless, powerful anesthetic sprayed over them in fine mist.

* * * *

The awakening was a complex one. It defied understanding. Und had evidently carried out his threat and with the medical machines at his command had created a masterpiece of surgery. The four former bodies were encompassed in one—apparently a fairly large human-looking body with a big head, but from the eyes of that head there looked out the Amazon, Abna, Viona, and Mexone, and in the brain of that body were four conflicting thought centers, each individual even yet, yet each one telepathic. When one of the former four moved, all had to move likewise. And, in concert, All-in-One got up from the surgery shelf and surveyed.

Once again the strange forces. All-in-One was shoved over the floor until it came finally to facing the twinkling green light atop its high tower— The cynical voice of Und boomed through the quiet.

"Well, my friends, how now? Do you feel better or worse for being molded into one being?"

The four made no answer. As yet they did not feel capable of one. The matter of answering—which in any case would have to be mentally—was a problem for four minds to agree upon before they could express themselves as one.

"No matter," Und said, as they remained silent. "I am satisfied that the experiment is justified. Now I shall return you to Xebar, my friends, where you will follow out the orders which are dictated to you, along with the rest of the slave population."

Again nameless forces came into action. To the vision of the All-in-One the vast machine room seemed to fade and was gradually replaced by the outlines of a space machine—the interior thereof. It was immediately recognizable as the machine in which they had made the outward journey from Xebar.

"So it was here all the time," came the mental voice of Abna, picked up instantly by the contiguous brains of the Amazon, Viona, and Mexone. "We were simply transferred from it by scientific means, and have been put back on it in the same way."

"And it is being guided by remote control back to Xebar," the Amazon commented. "As yet there is no mental compulsion at work on us because of the ship's insulation. We could, if we wished, and if we could reassemble the power plant, drive this machine to anywhere we wished without fear of mental domination."

"To what end?" asked the thoughts of Viona. "We would then have no chance of freeing ourselves from this preposterous body in which we're all imprisoned; and we'd certainly never find the *Ultra* again, granting it's still in existence."

"It's still in existence all right," the Amazon's thoughts responded. "It's too valuable in a thousand different ways for Und to destroy it. He gave himself away on that back in the laboratory."

"Then we go wherever the fates—or at any rate remote control—take us?" questioned the mind of Mexone.

"Certainly we do," Abna responded. "There may yet be a way of extricating ourselves—and the people of Xebar—from the mess we're in, and the only way to do it is to go forward."

There was a long interval as the All-in-One gazed through the observation window onto the void and the slowly growing disc that was Xebar. Then the thoughts of the Amazon came again.

"Come to think of it, if we ever have our normal bodies again, we've been given a great gift. Telepathy— henceforth we shall be able to add it to our qualifications. Our brains, separately or linked, will always retain that quality thanks to the ministrations of Und's mechanical surgeons."

"I don't think the telepathic gift will last once we have our own bodies back," Abna commented. "The different blood stream will probably negate the effect... But that's just conjecture at the moment. I wish I could feel as optimistic as you about getting our bodies back! All I foresee is the anger of Vax, Omnas, Kilas, and Jof when they know that their own bodies have gone forever and have been replaced by this cumbersome vestment which is nothing but a carrier for our linked brains."

"There is no reason why they should ever be told," came the thoughts of Mexone. "Their brains are in preservation, and they have no idea of what is going on. They can only find out the truth if at some time they have bodies again in which their brains can be placed. They have made a great sacrifice, and that their bodies have been lost is not our fault. Why tell them anything?"

"You mean," Abna asked, "write them down as heroes who made a great sacrifice in order to try and free their race?"

"Exactly. We'll find enough trouble without asking for it."

The subject was dropped, though the minds of the Amazon, Abna, and Viona were each thinking the same thing. Perhaps it *would* he as well never to reveal the truth—and in their state of eternal preserved unconsciousness the four men of Xebar would never know the real facts anyway. Until perhaps, some day, they chanced to find release...

Hours passed, and the planet of Xebar came nearer. But at least the hours were not passed in idleness. To the four chained as one in their ponderous physical body it was a time of regimentation of thought, a time of mutual question, argument, and agreement as to the best possible use they could make of the body that had been enforced upon them. And finally they reached agreement: Abna would do all the talking by thought transmission of course, and the other three minds would remain passive unless they detected some serious flaw or danger. Second, no sudden physical attack would be attempted unless agreed on beforehand by all four. And lastly they would all take care to guard their thoughts since, now they were telepaths, their minds would be nakedly open to the Xebarians. Not that this constituted a danger since the Xebarians were their friends, but just the same there could be some more disloyal than others. In any case there would be forewarning of this since, in being made telepaths, the Crusaders would be able to read the thoughts of others as well as have their own minds read…

And Xebar came nearer—and was finally reached without any help from the All-in-One. Controls moved themselves under the same uncanny remote control, which resulted finally in the vessel landing in a park-like space not very far from the great surgical building where their own bodies lay. Through the window many other space machines were visible, so presumably this was one of the planet's accepted spaceports.

The airlock opened automatically, and the thoughts of Abna were made manifest to the others.

"From here on, once deprived of the insulation of this ship, we shall be under mental control. I can suggest only one thing—fight that control with everything we've got."

Abna sensed the agreement to his suggestion—then the All-in-One stepped forth into the open, into the cloudy sunlight of the slave planet—and instantly, like an invisible clamp, there came a sense of hypnotic power, inflexibly commanding, telling them to go to a particular building in the city center. The All-in-One stood motionless, absorbing the commands but not immediately obeying them... Then came Abna's thoughts.

"Since we are being given individual orders it seems obvious that Und must have every being on the planet—and the other five planets as well—under separate mental control. It's not a case of mass compulsion for the multitude, but separate treatment for each unit. That's understandable, otherwise everybody would be doing the same thing. On the other hand it gives a glimpse of the enormous complication of Und's equipment."

"An order has been given us," came the thoughts of the Amazon. "To go to a certain building in the City center, the exact location of which will be revealed to us later... We can obey easily enough. On the other hand I detect the first flaw in Und's reasoning. There are four minds in this body—not one. And four have the will to resist, with all the power of four trained minds instead of one mind, docile from its creation."

"True enough," came the thoughts of Viona. "One thing Und did not reckon with: the opposition of four minds in union."

All four minds were silent for a moment, and the All-in-One stood motionless beside the spaceship. Then the voice-mind of Abna said:

"You are right, Vi. The mental compulsion is not strong enough to make four of us obey it simultaneously. We can—and will—defy it. But what will the consequences be? Und will surely know that his orders are not being obeyed."

"Yes, he'll probably know," the Amazon agreed, "but on the other hand what can he do about it? If he deserts his planet to come and investigate—an unlikely happening with his physical disability—he will also have to desert the mosaic of thought orders with which he controls these people, and those on the other worlds. I don't think he'll sacrifice his master-plan, if only temporarily, just because you're defying his compulsion. So far as he knows there's nothing we can do to upset things whether we defy his orders or not."

"Which is only too true," came Viona's thoughts, in regret.

"In that I don't concur," the Amazon responded. "I've just been thinking about something—the fact that the insulation of this planet's spaceships is so complete as to prevent thought waves from having any effect. What would the result be if the whole planet could have this insulation? Und would work in vain and the Xebarians would work on their own initiative, freed from his orders and domination."

"That," came the thoughts of Abna after due reflection, "is a marvelous idea, Vi. I must admit it had never occurred to me to utilize the insulation."

"There must be plenty of the material from which it is made," the Amazon continued, "otherwise spaceships would not be fitted with it so liberally. We have to discover where it is and devise the best means of using it. Our main difficulty will be getting the Xebarians themselves to see the point since they'll be under Und's domination. However, we'll find a way."

"But," Viona put in, "Und won't take a thing like that lying down. He'll know that his mental transmissions are somehow being blocked, and naturally he'll take retaliatory action."

"Mentally he'll be powerless, and if he tries something in physical action, using the machine world he controls, we'll think of an answer for him somehow. We've got this far, and we'll finish it."

"Which means that our immediate job is to find out where the ships' insulation comes from," came Abna's thoughts. "How do we begin?"

"We go amongst the people and take our chance." The Amazon thought for a moment and then continued, "A better idea, perhaps, would be to capture a few Xebarians and bring them into our spaceship here. Once inside it the insulation will cut off the mental compulsion and they'll be able to answer questions of their own free will... That's our line of action. Let's go."

The All-in-One began moving across the space grounds—slowly and ponderously, like some huge physical misfit. That at least was one advantage. The body which Und had selected to house their four brains was big in every way—far bigger than that of a normal Xebarian, and for that reason, a potential advantage.

As their body progressed they were conscious in their four minds of repetitive commands to report at a certain building in the city center, but as before they ignored it. It had no more strength than mere words against their combined mental rejection— Then suddenly their body was facing three Xebarians as they emerged from one of the many executive buildings around the space ground. They came to a sudden halt, regarding the huge creature lumbering towards them. They were obviously uncertain, and even afraid.

"Stop exactly where you are, my friends!" Abna's thoughts commanded—and at that the Xebarians stood waiting, their weird, mouthless faces expressionless.

"What do you want?" one of them demanded. "You seem like a stranger, judging from your physique. Yet I do not observe any alien spaceship."

The All-in-One moved nearer. The pin-head Xebarians still did not move, though the workings of their long fingers on huge hands betrayed the quality of their emotions.

"Who I am need not concern you, at the moment," Abna responded. "Suffice it that I wish to speak with you—in my own spaceship. You will not come to any harm. I assure you I am a friend of the Xebarians, and despite my physical vestment I am one of your race."

"None of us can believe that," came the curt reply.

"Nevertheless it is so. Let me mention the names of four of your race who are also my friends. You may know of them—Vax, Omnas, Kilas, and Jof. Vax is a space pilot amongst other things."

There came a slight relaxation of the hard barrier of opposing thoughts. The mention of the Xebarian names had obviously created an impression.

"I see you know the names," Abna hurried on, "Very well, let that be your assurance of my friendliness. Let us converse. My space machine is back there..." and the huge head nodded ponderously in its direction.

"It is not possible to comply with your request. We have other orders to fulfill."

"Orders of compulsion," Abna agreed. "I know about that. In this case you will ignore those orders."

"That is not possible. Further, though you have mentioned names that are familiar to us in this region, we do not trust you. Such of us can sense four minds at work in your strange body, and surely that is enough reason for us to distrust you—"

"This sort of thing isn't getting us anywhere, Abna," the Amazon's thoughts cut in abruptly. "Obviously they are not speaking their own minds, so they must be made to. We've got to act."

With that the All-in-One lunged forward, entirely under the major mental impulse of the Amazon herself. Abna, Viona, and Mexone had no chance to prevent the action: it came as something of a surprise—and in any case she was perhaps right.

There was nothing the three Xebarians could do with their delicate bodies. The All-in-One whirled them around and propelled them helplessly towards the waiting spaceship. They were bundled through the open airlock and into the control room, then the All-in-One depressed the switch which closed the airlock. The thick door closed instantly, which proved at least that remote control from Und's machines was no longer operating. Presumably he had removed the influence over the vessel once the All-in-One had stepped outside to the planet.

"Do you mind if I take over the questioning?" the Amazon's thoughts inquired. "There are times, Abna, when your own methods are too gentle—and we want action and plenty of it."

"Carry on," Abna's mind responded.

The All-in-One turned and looked at the three Xebarians standing by the observation window. It was obvious from their expressive eyes that they were scared, and considerably puzzled.

"Now," came the Amazon's thoughts, "perhaps we can communicate on more equal terms, my friends! In here you are insulated from the thought compulsion of your creator. You understand that?"

It was the one who had formerly communicated who answered. "Yes, we understand that. The insulation of the spaceship cuts off mental control. It is the same in every vessel."

"Exactly. And for that reason you are now able to speak your own minds. I repeat: I am your friend. And we need your help to free you from the domination of your creators. Presumably you prefer to do things of your initiative without being controlled?"

"Yes, that is so. But how can we help? To defy our creators is impossible. Their commands are too strong to be disobeyed."

"They're not at the moment, are they?"

"Not while insulation intervenes, no—but that cannot always be."

"I believe it can. Further, I believe it is the key to your freedom until your creator is placed in a position where he can control you no longer… To put it briefly, I am suggesting that every soul on this planet should be completely and absolutely insulated—and afterwards, the populations of the neighbor planets also."

There was definite interest in the thoughts of the three Xebarians: the Amazon could sense it, as also could Abna, Viona, and Mexone.

"But how would such a thing be possible?" the spokesman demanded. "Obviously it is impossible for us to live and work forever more within the protection of a spaceship—"

"Naturally—but buildings with roofs of insulation, and portable dwellings and vehicles, also with insulated tops is not beyond the bounds of possibility… I am talking about the materials from which spaceship insulation is made. Can it be gained easily? Is it manufactured, or is it a natural product of Xebar?"

"The ingredients of the insulation are natural—and there are three of them; but the final process is manufactured. To make the sheets of insulation we use the bark of *linip* trees; a malleable kind of metal called *zanrith*, and finally a kind of paste compound which is extracted from the ground itself—*ergotax* by name."

"And the result is a sheet of insulation which can be cut and molded into any form?" the Amazon asked.

"That is so, and there is an abundance of linip,

zanrith and ergotax. What do you suggest?"

"At first I thought of buildings and movable vehicles, but now I realize how malleable this stuff is I am inclined to revise my opinion. Perhaps helmets would be more to the point..." The Amazon mentally consulted with Abna, Viona and Mexone on this point, then she resumed, "Yes, helmets would answer the case perfectly and they would not in any way interfere with your movements."

"You mean equip every soul on this planet with helmets, regardless of the immense diversity of head shapes?" the Xebarian spokesman asked dubiously. "That will not be an easy task."

"Not easy, I admit, but on the other hand not impossible."

"I can see the benefit," the spokesman said, "but it will not be possible for us to secure the various ingredients for you. As soon as we step into the open we shall again be under control and unable to help you, or show you anything."

"You can leave that part to me," the Amazon said. "I know how to fight the mental compulsion, whereas you do not. As for showing us where the various materials are, and the factory that can handle their manufacture, that is easier than you think... I notice you have an instrument there in your belt, rather like a knife. May I borrow it for a moment?"

Convinced that nothing menacing was implied, the spokesman handed it over. The All-in-One took the instrument, examined the sharp, squat blade, and then dug it forcibly into the spongy inner gray coating with which the spaceship was lined. A rip, a few twists, and a jagged square of the stuff came away, looking and feeling exactly like asbestos.

"There you are," the Amazon said, as with unaccustomed hands she fashioned a rough hood. "Wear that, my friend, night and day, and no outside influence will trouble you."

The Xebarian took the stuff, shaping and twisting it in his own hands, adding the necessary modifications—until at last the hood was reasonably well fitting. He placed it on his head and the quality of his thoughts showed his satisfaction. "Why such an idea never occurred to me I don't know," he confessed. "But then it hardly could. Outside 1 am always under compulsion and have not time for such thoughts… But what of my friends?"

"How come we can still pick up his thoughts now?" Mexone asked, puzzled. "If the cap is such an effective insulator it should work both ways, surely?"

"You're forgetting that the source of this man's thoughts is directly under his cap—hence they can still get through," the Amazon responded. "But anything from a greater distance is cut off…" she turned again to the Xebarian. "As for your friends, that is up to them…" The knife was handed back. "You seem to know most of the details I want so it is only with you that I need be concerned. If your friends wish to convert some of this inner insulation lining to their own uses I shall certainly have no objection. They'll simply be getting

rough helmets ahead of the proper ones, that' s all…
And by the way, what is your name? It would be as
well for me to know it."

"My name is Tulan, and my occupation that of engineer."

"Good… Very well, then—let's get busy. Show me
where the insulation ingredients are to be found and
manufactured."

"For that we shall need this vessel—and you must
fly it as I direct."

The All-in-One did not query the point. The space
machine was quickly raised to a height of a thousand feet over the city, then under Tulan's directions
it moved forward, slowing its pace as it crossed the
network of the city center. Tulan pointed below to a
group of buildings, all connected to each other by
means of metal bridges at roof-level.

"Those are the factories," he explained. "Insulation
material is not the only thing they manufacture, of
course. There are all kinds of textiles and fabrics
undergoing process… But that is the building with
which you will be directly concerned."

"And you, my friend," the Amazon added, "naturally I am looking to you to lend your aid, which you
can without outside compulsion influencing you."

"I will do everything possible," Tulan promised.
"Now, move on, again, and I will show you where the
actual ingredients are to be found."

This proved a fairly long job. First a journey of a
hundred miles to a forest of queer-looking trees—actu-

ally the linip trees whose bark was an essential factor in the insulating formula... Then on again in a wide detour to a mining area where amongst other things, zanrith was being produced—the second element. And lastly to a deserted area that looked like a mud-swamp, a yellow oozing morass similar to that in which the fantastic fruit trees grew. This was where the paste-compound—ergotax—was extracted from, to form the third ingredient.

"That is the sum total," Tulan said, when the survey was over. "What are your immediate plans—and what do you, wish me to do?"

The Amazon replied, "I want you, by any means you care to adopt, to secure the necessary labor to extract the three ingredients from the different areas as fast as possible. I want you also to have all the stuff transported to the factory for processing. You will delegate men you can trust—these two here for instance—indicating the two men by the wall—to the task of setting up parties to determine the size of heads of everybody in the population. I for my part will go amongst the people and explain why this is being done, and I'll explain to them that it is the only way to throw off the yoke of Und and regain—or rather have, for the first time—natural independence..."

"I will do my best," Tulan promised. "And of course I am never to remove this insulated hood—until I have a properly manufactured one?"

"That is correct. It would be an advantage if you made rough hoods for your two friends here... One other thing, this space ship, when I have again brought it down to its former position, will always be our base of operations, to which you will report from time to time… Everything clear? Any questions?"

"Yes. What happens if our creators discover what we are doing? There may be a tragic price to pay for refusal to obey orders."

"Leave me to deal with that," the Amazon said. "I know more about the circumstances than you do."

"Very well. There was also mention, when we first communicated, of extending our activities to the other planets. What have you in mind for that?"

"Many things," the Amazon responded. "We'll attend to that when we come to it. For the moment I am returning to base, and then we can commence operations."

CHAPTER 8

MENTAL COMPULSION

Once the Amazon, Abna, Viona and Mexone had launched their campaign there was surprisingly little opposition to it. They moved about the people of the teeming city, four highly trained minds in a ridiculous and cumbersome body—and they talked, cajoled, and explained. Usually they won their point—stressing it by every means of modern communication that the Xebarians possessed. Ultra radio—which made communication possible over a wide area by transmitting thought-waves instead of voices, newssheets, which conveyed in writing everything that was required, and finally telepathic television, by which the thought-waves of the person transmitted—in this case the All-in-One—were quite comprehensible to the millions of viewers on the planet.

The theme which the sleepless, never-hungry, never-tired All-in-One plugged relentlessly through many Earth weeks was independence. This was the one element that the Xebarians had never known since the day of their creation. They were by instinct a race of decent, progressive people, in spite of their queer physique, and as such had every right to pursue their own lives in their own way without being forced mercilessly to prepare the way for the rehabilitation of a planet infinitely far away, and of which they knew nothing. True, Und had created them, but that did not give him the right to rule them eternally thereafter, any more than a child of natural parents should be ruled ruthlessly throughout the rest of its existence. This facet of the matter was not unduly emphasized—chiefly because the Xebarians knowing nothing of sex, would not understand.

Gradually, steadily, through the weeks, it became obvious that the campaign was bearing fruit, the hardest opposition being that of mental control from Und himself. But once the labor crews at the three 'ingredient' sites were equipped with rough hoods—and the factory bosses likewise—things took on a different aspect. They felt what it was like to have real independence and strove mightily to retain it. Helmets began to be manufactured in the thousands; a well-planned organization saw to it that they were delivered where they were most needed—and the greater the distribution the less Xebarians there were under the influence...

Slowly but surely through many weary weeks, the battle was being won. Pin-heads, big-heads, bladder-heads, pole-heads—all types were being equipped with helmets at the rate of thousands every tine Xebar performed a revolution.

It was when the last hundred thousand of Xebarians remained to be equipped that the All-in-One relaxed their efforts. As far as Xebar was concerned the battle was won. All but a tenth of the planet's population were thinking their own thoughts, were independent and entirely free. Particularly were they loyal to the queer, lumbering being who, throughout, had appeared unaffected by the waves of compulsion surrounding the planet.

It was time, the four minds in one body decided, to try and seek once again their natural forms and be rid of the juggernaut in which they were imprisoned. To this end they went to the surgical laboratory and spent several days studying the design—and set-up of the surgical monster on wheels, which had performed the original operation. When at length they felt confident enough, and had made several experimental tests, they submitted their cumbersome body to its ministrations, passing into unconsciousness as they saw their own limp bodies being carried by the mechanical giant from out of the adjoining anteroom.

Perhaps an hour—perhaps a day, they did not know which, and the fogs of the anesthetic began to disperse, leaving them to awaken to the glorious feeling of limbs, organs, enormous strength, and most glorious of all—oneness. No longer four brains linked Siamese-fashion to each other, but distinct and individual.

"That feels better," the Amazon said, as she levered her lithe, gloriously perfect body from one of the operating shelves. "Just like coming out of prison."

Abna's answer came in her mind: not a spoken one. "I'm inclined to agree with you, Vi. But don't forget the one advantage we've gained. At the moment we're telepaths as well—and the uses of that gift—which Und's surgical machines conferred upon us—may be numerous as time goes on. I don't know how long the effect will last, however, now that our brains are being fed and nourished by our human bloodstream."

"Well, let's enjoy it whilst we can—it even makes it unnecessary to speak," Viona remarked, standing up; to which Mexone replied,

"A handier way of exchanging opinions and plans without opening one's mouth I can't imagine."

"There is also the drawback," Abna said grimly. "'Being telepaths our minds are now completely open to Und's persuasion until we get helmets to protect ourselves... I don't know about any of you, but I can already feel his influence beginning to penetrate."

Now he came to mention it the fact was obvious. In the un-insulated area of the surgery there was a growing conviction of compulsion—as yet hazy orders to do certain things. And—strangely enough there was a distinct flavor of venom in the thoughts. In a rapid space of time the influence would become stronger and finally, unless protection were sought, be beyond defiance.

"The four of us in unison could defeat the influence," the Amazon said. "Individually, it is nearly impossible—or will be when our minds are adjusted and 'soaked' in the compulsion... We've got to get hoods quickly. Let's be on our way."

She turned towards the doorway, then Abna restrained her.

"Just a minute, Vi. What about the four men who loaned us their bodies? They can never have their bodies back, thanks to Und, but surely we ought to do something?"

"There isn't time with this mental compulsion growing upon us."

"We must *make* time, and repay the debt we owe. I see only one thing for it—let those four isolated brains take over this juggernaut body we've been using. We can set the controls to have all four brains linked up. That's the best we can do. I've no doubt that, in time, Vax, Omnas, Kilas and Jof will find a solution for themselves. Give me a hand to adjust the machine."

This was duly done, and as quickly as possible because the inflowing power of compulsion was becoming a definite, even a deadly thing. Once the machine was adjusted Abna went quickly to the ante-room and brought forth the four cylinders of cloudy fluid in which were preserved the brains of the Xebarians. He placed them beside the 'juggernaut' on the operating shelf and then switched on the master-machine.

"That ought to do it." he said, as the others glanced at him. "The machine is correctly adjusted to do the job. Now let's get out of here."

They departed immediately; then as they came to the outdoors without even the protection of the building, which to a certain extent mitigated the effect of external mental influence, they felt the full force of the compulsion waves streaming across space from Und's uncanny machines. It gave them a rough idea of the power under which Xebarians had been laboring until the helmets had saved them. Suggestions, homicidal and murderous, began to make definite inroads into their minds.

"We've got to fight this thing until we can get to the factory and get helmets," Abna said, turning a strained face. "I think we can take it as certain that somehow, Und knows exactly what we are doing—knows even that we have managed to defeat him so far and have encouraged the Xebarians to do the same. You can sense the venom in his thoughts and particularly the urge to murderous intent which can have disastrous consequences for us if we're not very careful."

The Amazon only nodded, her thoughts, telepathically conveyed, were enough in themselves to show the chaos of mind she was enduring.

"And while we're standing here things are getting worse," Viona said. "Let's get to the factory whilst we can."

She underlined her words by seizing the Amazon's and Abna's arms and impelling them down the steps of the building. For the moment she was perhaps the clearest thinker of them all, and most certainly she appreciated the danger. With Mexone coming up behind she practically forced her father and mother to the factory, through streets busy with hooded Xebarians who gaped at the—to them—four staggering strangers in the last stages of mental control.

The factory was reached, and for the four their surroundings had ceased to have sensible meaning. With everything they had got they were fighting the urge to turn on each other and destroy.

"Hoods!" Viona gasped out to a surprised foreman. "Hoods far all of us… Any size as long as they cover our heads. Quickly—"

Four hoods were whipped from overstocked shelves and slipped in place. The four stood trembling, the compulsion flooding away from them in an ebbing tide. Their faces wet with perspiration from the mental effort they had put up they finally looked at each other.

"Well, we managed it," Abna said finally. "Thanks to Viona keeping her control to the last moment."

"Good job I did!" Viona said, adjusting the hood more comfortably on her copper-golden hair. "Und seems to be turning the heat on us with no uncertain power—"

"Who are you four?" demanded the factory foreman abruptly, his thoughts plainly suspicious. "I provided you with hoods because I saw the situation was desperate—but I would like an explanation."

"Easily given," Abna smiled. "We are the four responsible for your present freedom. We've now abandoned the single clumsy body in which you saw us and have restored ourselves to normal. In doing that we nearly fell under the mental influence…"

"The four who call themselves the Cosmic Crusaders?"

"The same," the Amazon agreed. "We were—" She paused and turned towards the doorway as a pinheaded figure in a hood came in.

"Tulan!" Abna exclaimed in delight. "Welcome, my friend."

The friendly Xebarian looked at them in vague puzzlement.

"We are the four minds which you at first detected in that clumsy body," the Amazon explained. "We have just restored ourselves to normal in the surgical laboratory."

"Ah! I begin to understand..." Tulan's thoughts began to flow more freely. "At first I was mystified—but now I read the real circumstances from your mind... I am glad I have found you," he hurried on. "I went to the base spaceship to find you but discovered you had gone. Your mental waves, which I managed to pick up, seemed to suggest you might be in, this direction, so I came—"

"Have you something to report?" Abna interrupted.

"I have indeed. Disquieting news, my friends... A little while ago three of our friends, who so far have not been provided with hoods, died. The mental compulsion effect has been so tremendously increased that it brings death."

"That is only to be expected," the Amazon said swiftly. "The Lords of Creation evidently realizing that we are defying them, so things are being made difficult for the few who as yet are not adequately safeguarded."

"But that is not all," Tulan's thoughts hurried on. "Before they died each of our three friends revealed something of what the Lords of Creation intend to do in reprisal against us. Since three men heard mentally the same thing it cannot be put down to the ravings of one alone."

"Well?" the Amazon demanded. "What kind of reprisal is threatening?"

"Mental compulsion on a scale never before dreamed of, powerful enough perhaps to even penetrate the insulation we have devised. And the orders will not be as they have been in the past: they will concentrate only on destruction. That means that each will destroy the other. Our peoples will be destroyed, and what survivors there are will be lost in eternal madness."

"So that's it," Abna muttered, casting a brief look at the Amazon. "Maybe it will penetrate the insulation, and maybe not. Depends on how much power is used by Und, who evidently has only been working on a small percentage of the power possible up to now. I think our insulation will hold—but what of the other five planets who have no protection at all? Their peoples will all be converted into homicidal maniacs, and inevitably they'll fly here and create wholesale destruction."

"It's simply vicious spite, the whole thing!" Viona declared. "Now he knows the races he has created are trying to cut free of him, and his rehabilitation ideas, he seeks to destroy them."

"And I am afraid he will succeed," Tulan added. "His thoughts conveyed the impression that if his mental powers don't produce the effect he desires when at full strength he'll resort to material means and destroy every planet and the sun which shines upon them. Naturally not a being will be left."

"Yes, I suppose he could do that with the machines he has, just as easily as he first created the system and its sun," Abna muttered.

"The thoughts implied one machine in particular," Tulan's thoughts hurried on. "I have never heard of such a machine. The Zero-Thought Amplifier."

Abna gave a start find looked quickly at the Amazon. Her lips tightened in sudden alarm. Tulan, reading their thoughts, looked from one to the other.

"I notice that causes you considerable alarm," he commented. "Might I ask why?"

"The Zero-Thought Amplifier is the most destructive machine ever conceived," the Amazon told him. "There is no form of matter which can stand against it. A thought is concentrated into it, a thought having the mathematical equation of zero-negative. In consequence, all forms of matter within range—and the range can extend to millions of miles—cease to be! No confusion, no debris, not even a speck of dust. Planets, suns, people—all vanish."

"And that is what we're facing?" Tulan demanded, horrified.

"Yes," Abna told him, grimly. "That is unless we think mighty fast and beat him to it." He pondered for a moment, and then: "You say you got the impression that he would only use the Amplifier if his increased mental compulsion failed?"

"So I understood."

"In that case," the Amazon said, looking at Abna, "we're facing danger from two directions. The increase in compulsion may not overcome the Xebarians, but will certainly lash the populations of the remaining five planets to violence, severely enough to cause the decimation of the populations and ourselves included. It may take them centuries to recover from it—and our sole object is to give all of them peace and freedom. If on the other hand, the increase in compulsion doesn't work we'll face destruction from the Amplifier which will be absolute."

"Yes," Abna agreed slowly. "That seems to be the situation. There's an interesting sidelight on it too. Either Und has built an Amplifier according to the formula we gave him, or else the original one aboard the *Ultra* never really disappeared any more than the ship itself did, and he's planning on using that."

"Then why did he go to the trouble of torturing me to get the formula?" Viona, demanded.

Abna shrugged. "There might be two reasons. One—because at heart Und is obviously a sadist and enjoyed making you suffer; and two—he perhaps needed the safeguard of having the formula in case something went wrong when he tried to restore the Amplifier and the *Ultra*."

"Whatever the side issues, we've got to act fast," the Amazon said, pondering. "We could perhaps launch an all-out physical attack with weapons on Und—

using every space machine in the Xerbarian fleet for the purpose, but there again we'd have no certainty of victory while he has the Amplifier with which to destroy us... I think the better way would be to equip the populations of the five remaining worlds with hoods as fast as ever possible. At least it might serve to save them and us from catastrophe. If that succeeds we'll have to consider an all-out attack afterwards and risk the Amplifier destroying us."

"It would seem to be the only course," Tulan agreed, following her thoughts. "Having got this far to freedom I myself am willing to take any risk, and I think I speak for my fellows."

"What kind of people are they on the neighbor worlds?" the Amazon asked.

"Same as ourselves, and about at the same stage of scientific development."

"As yet they know nothing about this struggle for freedom," the Amazon continued. "They don't know that three quarters of the race of this world have been freed. How will they react when they learn that we wish to 'enforce' the same freedom on them?"

"They'll react favorably." There was complete confidence in Tulan's thoughts. "I know the leading figures on each planet. Many times we have communicated and visited, but at that time it was to further our mutual plans as dictated by Und. I think I can persuade them that independence is more preferable and have them turn their various resources to the manufacture of insulating hoods."

"Then don't waste any time," the Amazon said. "Go immediately and see what can be done. You know how desperately urgent the situation is. We for our part will speed up our own hood manufacture in every possible way to take care of the remainder of the Xebarian population."

Tulan's thoughts ceased. He hurried out of the building, full of the urgency of his mission...

* * * *

It did not take the Crusaders long to get themselves organized. The first thing they had to do was satisfy the hooded nuclear beings of Xebar that they were really the same persons as the solitary juggernaut individual who had earlier brought them independence—and as it happened they got complete confirmation of their assertion by reason of the fact that the original Juggernaut man came into their midst, housing the brains of Vax, Omnas, Kilas, and Jof. The surgical wizardry had been successfully completed and, although not entirely satisfied with the result, the four Xebarians bore out the Crusadersl story and offered themselves as willing helpers in whatever new plan they intended to follow.

There remained only one second personal problem— and that was food and drink, Possessing their own bodies again, the quartet were naturally at the mercy of these two factors. The Juggernaut himself took care of this, making arrangements with a synthesis factory for food to be manufactured—along with drink—in unlimited quantities from basic chemicals.

Then, their physical cravings satisfied for the time being, the four went into action, with Juggernaut helping wherever he could. All four of them went in different directions—Juggernaut remaining in the city center—speeding up the manufacture and distribution of hoods by one, two, and three hundred percent. Juggernaut, for its part, was supplied with a hood early on and promptly rendered immune from the mental disturbances. Not that they had been causing him— or them—any undue trouble since once again the four brains in unison formed a formidable barrier. However, as the power of compulsion steadily increased there remained the possibility of trouble.

Days passed. The thousands of the Xebarian population remaining un-hooded were duly cared for. Everything was swept aside solely for this purpose— and with the days the increase of mental power became gradually noticeable. In consequence, hundreds of as yet un-hooded Xebarians killed themselves, or each other, or else died of violent convulsions following complete mental derangement...

Days became weeks and, checking up on the figures, the Crusaders discovered that every being on Xebar was accounted for. True, a few hundreds had died, but in the vast majority there was security. Hood distribution was complete. Every being on the planet had one, sheltering under its security, wondering—as did the Crusaders themselves—whether this was only a respite or whether, as the inflowing compulsion reached maximum the hoods would not provide enough insulation.

Into the midst of this precarious situation Tulan returned from his tour of the five neighbor worlds. Immediately he joined the Crusaders and Juggernaut in the space machine that they were still using as their base headquarters, Abna having had the vessel over-hauled to disconnect the remote control apparatus Und had earlier employed. It was immediately obvious from Tulan's thoughts that he had a good deal about which to be pleased.

"The maximum, effort is being exerted," he 'said.' "I have explained the details to those who matter on each planet, and the result has been a complete turn over to hood manufacture—for which, of course, there are the necessary ingredients on each world. My biggest ally was the increase in mind force and the change of orders to homicidal compulsion. From that occurrence our friends of the neighbor worlds know that something is not as it should be... Unfortunately, hundreds are dying and being killed in the areas where hoods have not yet been provided, but that we cannot help. The greater part of each population will be made immune..." Tulan's thoughts paused; and then, "The only point is: for how long?"

"Meaning what?" the Amazon asked.

"Well, surely it is obvious to you that compulsion has not yet reached maximum? When it does so, will the hoods stand it? And if they do, what will Und do next? This expectation of annihilation at any moment is terribly unnerving."

"In that I agree," the Amazon replied. "However, it will interest you to know, Tulan, that the laboratories have devised a detector, which marks for us on a needle the intensity of compulsion flowing in from outer space. It has been increasing for many weeks now... When it remains constant we can safely assume that the maximum power is being exerted."

Tulan's thoughts were puzzled. "Why doesn't Und use the maximum all at once instead of building up to it?"

"May be a variety of reasons," the Amazon responded. "The most likely explanation is that his apparatus builds up by stages to the peak, as do most electrical machines."

"And when it reaches maximum we can expect trouble?" the Juggernaut asked. "It's plain that none of the populations will be reacting as Und expects, and that gives him ample reason for using the Zero-Thought Amplifier!"

The Amazon was on the point of replying when Abna stopped her.

"I believe," he said slowly, "that there may be a way to tackle this business. First, let's consider the essential point: we want to destroy Und and all he stands for, don't we?"

"Nothing would give me greater satisfaction, or the inhabitants of these six planets more cause for rejoicing," the Amazon replied.

"Very well. Consider this for a proposition: The way things are going it's more than likely, as Juggernaut has said, that Und will use the Zero-Thought Amplifier. That we've got to stop at all costs. Now, it's unlikely he'll use it until the mental power has reached maximum and he has had time to study results. Right?"

"Right," the Amazon agreed.

"That may give us a few days in which to turn round—"

"Maybe only a few hours," Viona interrupted. "There's no way of telling when maximum will be reached."

"All right then: say a few hours. It will take him some time after that to decide whether to use the Amplifier or not, align it up, and so forth. In that time we've got to get to him, and completely destroy him."

"We thought of that before," the Amazon pointed out. "The trouble is that he'll spot us coming and use the Amplifier on us—with disastrous consequences."

"That's the point I want to make," Abna said quietly. "I'm right in thinking, am I not, that the Zero-Amplifier works on the direct beam principle? That is, it concentrates a beam, in the confines of which are the thought waves to be projected?"

The Amazon frowned a little. "Yes, that's right. But how—?"

"The fact that it works on the beam principle instead of dissipating itself in concentric rings which radiate in all sides from the source may be our saving factor," Abna hurried on. "It means, to cut a long story short, that we can approach Und's planet by the 'back door,' so to speak."

Neither the Amazon, Viona or Mexone made any comment. They just waited for the next, still not sure what Abna was driving at.

"We can take a well prepared armada," Abna continued. "We'll set off into space in a wide circle and approach Und's planet from the rear, as it faces Xebar. If he's got the Thought Amplifier lined up for the destruction of this system he won't be able to suddenly switch round and concentrate on us. As we know, that kind of maneuver takes a considerable time..." Abna paused and then finished, "What I am reckoning on is that, from the time of Und locating our armada in space to the time it would take him to obliterate us, we'll have reached him. I know it's a gamble, but things have got to the stage where we've got to take one."

"And the chances are that we'll pull it off," the Amazon said, thinking. "True, he may have weapons of terrific power apart from the Zero Amplifier with which to wipe us out, but we'll have to chance it... As far as his compulsion efforts are concerned we'll be all right in a spaceship since the insulation will be doubled with our hoods as well." She moved resolutely. "Right! We'll have an armada assembled right away: you can arrange that, Tulan. And you, Juggernaut, see the controller of ultra radio and tell him to advise us, in space, when the maximum has been reached on the thought-detector...

"And for us four," the Amazon concluded, looking at Viona, Mexone, and Abna, "there remains only the task of loading the selected ships with provisions...

Then we're away, and if the chance should come to pay Und in full for the way he treated Viona in the early stages I'll readily take it!"

"I wonder if you would?" Viona asked surprisingly, her voice quiet. "A woman of your strength against a legless man? Somehow I think that incident against me had better be forgotten, mother."

* * * *

Six hours later the machines were ready—two hundred of the fastest Xebar could muster, and all of them armed with deadly scientific weapons. Yet, oddly enough, there was not one nuclear bomb even though the inhabitants of Xebar and the neighboring worlds were themselves nuclear. Apparently nuclear physics was not something on which they had concentrated unduly... As far as armadas from the other planets in the system were concerned, the Amazon—who had taken charge of operations—was not particularly concerned. Two hundred machines could do a terrible lot of damage—and besides the people of the neighbor worlds had their hands full already in the manufacture of hoods, without having to concentrate on and equip a space-armada.

It was approximately at the hour chosen for departure, when the Crusaders, together with Tulan and Juggernaut, were already in their machines that there came an ultra radio message transmitting the customary thought waves.

"Urgent communication for the Golden Amazon..."

The Amazon switched on the apparatus, already aware of what was coming.

"Amazon speaking. Proceed with message…"

"I have a report that the compulsion detector has remained unchanged for the past twenty four hours and therefore may be considered to have reached maximum."

"Right…" The Amazon stared thoughtfully in front of her. "Thank you. Over and out."

She switched off and looked at the others. The faces reflected thoughts that were pretty much her own.

"We'd better get on our way as fast as we can," Abna said urgently, turning to the control board. "The one main enemy now is time—whether we can get to Und's planet soon enough."

"Anyway," came the combined thoughts of Juggernaut, "we can be satisfied on one thing. Obviously Und's maximum compulsion attempt isn't good enough. He still hasn't broken down the resistance of the hoods."

The Amazon nodded slowly, gazing through the observation window onto the Xebarians, hooded and active, outside. They were quite undisturbed by the enormous force of compulsion that was in existence all around them.

"All right, what are we waiting for?" the Amazon asked abruptly. "Let's be on our way… Okay, Abna, give her everything she's got."

He nodded, moved to the control board, and switched on the power plant. Then he transferred the power to the jets and instantly the vessel began climbing with dizzying speed, sending Tulan and Juggernaut staggering for a moment under the force of the acceleration. It only lasted for a few moments during the initial outward rush from Xebar, then once the planet had been left behind and the void reached the velocity decreased to produce the effect of normal gravity.

"Anywhere from this moment on we can expect trouble," the Amazon mused, glancing first at the armada to the rear and then towards the distant, looming planet of Und. "Fast though we're traveling Und may catch up on us."

"Not if we can help it," Abna answered grimly; and he began the adjustment of controls, which resulted in the vessel heading at right angles to Und's planet—into the depths of space. This was all part of the 'detour' plan. Presently the returning curve in space would be made, resulting in the vessels approaching Und's planet from the side beyond its orbit.

And, undisturbed, the progress continued. The Amazon took up her usual position by the observation window, her violet eyes studying the void in general und Und's planet in particular. After a moment Viona and Mexone crossed to her. In silence they surveyed the planet and the four poised magnetic balls still in position about it.

"Suspiciously quiet, if you ask me," Viona commented. "I'll wager there are plenty of fireworks soon—probably when we get nearer the planet."

"If so, we're ready for them." The Amazon glanced

briefly at the armaments lined round the walls of the space machine. "We may walk into death at the end with Und's superior equipment, but we'll certainly give a spectacular account of ourselves before that happens."

"How long is it likely to take before we reach the planet?" Mexone asked, and it was Abna who answered him from the switchboard.

"Around six hours. I'm using the maximum velocity possible—within the limits of personal comfort, that is."

Silence again. The absolute lack of attack was somehow more unnerving than an out and out onslaught. It seemed strange that, with the weapons and instruments at his command, Und had not sighted the armada by this time. He did not even need to see it telescopically, instruments would show its position in space and reveal the fact that it was coming ever nearer. The only assumption that could be gathered was that he *did* know, but was waiting his chance to spring a devastating surprise...

When three hours had passed the vessels were well out to the 'rear' of Und's planet. Only then did Abna alter course and begin the inward journey—and the alertness of the Amazon, Viona and Vexone, and for that matter Tulan and Juggernaut as well, increased correspondingly. Surely, with two hundred machines bearing down now directly on his planet, Und would act. Once an actual landing was made he would not perhaps have the same opportunity—

But still nothing happened, and the looming world with its patchwork surface and curiously rosy hue swept ever nearer.

"I don't understand it!" the Amazon confessed, staring through the window. "I just don't understand it. I hardly expected the Zero-Amplifier, though it was certainly on the cards—but I did expect perhaps disintegrating rays or heat beams. There's nothing—and I don't like it. Not even a radio message of warning!"

"Well," Abna said, still at the controls, "If we're walking into a trap—the same as we did when we first arrived—we'll have to think our way out when we're in it…" He paused and gave a significant glance as with a sudden scream the space machine contacted the first layer of atmosphere. Thereafter it was only a matter of minutes, the speed constantly decreasing, before the vessel reached the planet's surface—and the Amazon gave a wry smile as she realized that this was the first time a landing on this world had ever been made in the normal way.

On the previous occasions there had been a mysterious transportation to Und's master laboratory while the travelers were still in space… Strange, very strange, that Und had this time allowed an actual landing to be made.

"Where exactly we are I don't know," Abna confessed, moving the switch that controlled the airlock. "As near as I could I dropped us in a clear space in a wilderness of machines…" He stood waiting as the airlock opened. When it had moved aside to its fullest extent there loomed a vision outside of tall, inexplicable machines with an avenue of glittering metal dividing them, stretching away in a flawlessly straight line to a solitary tower, on top of which glowed a familiar green light.

"Well, you didn't do badly, Abna," the Amazon remarked rather dryly, heading towards the opening. "There's our destination—if we ever reach it."

She stepped outside into the weird ruby-purple light and waited for the others to follow her. Then she glanced up at the vision of the armada circling and descending to wherever they could find a resting place amidst the huge machinery.

"If he's going to spring a surprise he'll have to do it quickly," Abna commented, as they began to move forward. "We're nearly on top of him as it is."

"Do you think," Viona asked slowly, "that for some reason he's deserted the planet?"

"What should he want to do that for?" the Amazon demanded. "He's got everything he needs here, and vast plans to fulfill."

"Then why doesn't he attack us? He must know by this time that we're here."

The Amazon did not respond. She simply did not know the answer. With Abna by her side she went on steadily along the avenue of metal, glancing back once to see Tulan, Juggernaut, and dozens of the nuclear race all following behind—every one ready for trouble, every one hooded, as of course were the Crusaders themselves.

Then suddenly when they were perhaps a hundred yards from the site of the green light tower, the Amazon came to a stop and gripped Abna's arm. Her voice when she spoke was tense with excitement.

"Look! The *Ultra*!"

Up to this point the enormous bulk of the space machine had been hidden by the even greater proportions of the machines around it—but here, at this particular point, the *Ultra* was just commencing to come into view. There was no doubt about that polished, tapering nose.

The Amazon did not wait to ask questions. She began hurrying towards it—until Abna caught up with her and grasped her arm. "Wait a minute, Vi! This may be the trap we've been expecting. What more likely to attract us than the *Ultra*?"

The Amazon pulled free. "Trap or otherwise, I'm going to satisfy myself."

And she went forward again actively, dodging around and between the great machines on every hand—until at length she came to the comparatively clear space where the colossal space cruiser stood, fitting exactly into an area where there were machines on every hand.

The Amazon slowed down in her rush, her eyes quickly passing over the old, familiar lines. A home had been returned—the only link to both Earth and sanity across untold light centuries. But why? What was the machine doing here?

"I don't like it!" Abna muttered, coming to her side. "I'm still sure it's a trap. Even the airlock's open! It certainly wasn't when we were mysteriously spirited away from it."

The Amazon hesitated, her mind searching for the answer to quite a lot of puzzling questions. One thing seemed clear: the *Ultra* had probably been guided from outer space to its present position by the machines of this fantastic planet, under Und's control—long after the Crusaders had been taken from it. But why the open airlock? As Abna had said, it had been hermetically shut when he, the Amazon, Viona and Mexone had been taken from it.

"Only one answer," the Amazon said at length. "Und must have opened it, for some reason or other—" She stopped and then gave an exclamation. "Of course! So he could get at the Zero-Thought Amplifier! Trap or no trap I'm going to investigate."

She went forward resolutely, Abna and the others a little way behind her. Reaching the open airlock she hesitated for a moment, grimly aware of the fact that she had no weapons with which to protect herself— Then she went on again, through the narrow passageway which led through the air-conditioning chamber, and so into the control room, that old familiar control room with its wealth of scientific machines and weapons.

She stopped in the doorway—amazed. Abna cane up behind her and a low whistle of astonishment escaped him.

"Und! By all that's incredible!"

"And from the look of him he's dead," the Amazon added grimly.

She advanced again. At the far side of the control room, mounted on a tripod with a universal turntable, stood the box-like apparatus that was the most devastating of all weapons—the Zero-Thought Amplifier. Before it, motionless on one of the *Ultra*'s moveable chairs, sat the last legless survivor of Valdon. One hand was extended towards, but not quite touching, the small switch-panel of the Amplifier. The forearm rested on the edge of the tripod turntable and apparently it was the only thing acting as a support to Und.

The Amazon reached him, pushed one of his shoulders gently, then watched him reel out of the chair and crash with dead weight to the floor. He remained motionless curiously rigid, amber-irised eyes staring sightlessly at the ceiling.

Immediately Abna went down on his knees and made a brief examination. The Amazon, Viona, and Mexone watched him intently, as did Tulan, Juggernaut, and the other Xebarians crowding through the airlock.

"Dead," Abna pronounced at length, with an amazed look. "But don't ask me why."

The Amazon stood in puzzled silence for a moment, then struck with a thought she experimentally raised the hood from about her head and prepared herself for a mental shock. None came.

"It's over," she said, tossing the hood on one side. "There's no mental compulsion at work any more."

"Naturally not with Und dead," Abna replied, casting aside his own hood. "But how did it happen? Nobody could attack him; we didn't do anything, and his death from heart failure is most unlikely. It looks as if he was on the very verge of switching on the Amplifier when death overtook him..."

The Amazon did not seem to be listening. She crossed swiftly to the radio equipment and switched it on. With perfect familiarity she tuned in quickly to the wavelength that would contact her with Xebar; then she spoke into the microphone.

"The Golden Amazon calling Xebar. Listen carefully. I am now on the planet of Und. We have arrived safely, along with the rest of the armada. For a reason we haven't yet found, Und—the so-called leader of the mythical Lords of Creation—is dead. And apparently the planets only escaped annihilation by a hair's breadth. We have yet to find why Und died, but in the meantime it would appear that compulsion has ended for ever... Listen now carefully to my instructions. This radio cannot receive a reply from you because it is not designed for receiving telepathic waves—and we do not wish to return to our Xebarian spaceship to receive a message from you. So, to overcome the difficulty use two taps on the microphone to signify 'Yes' and one tap to signify No.' If you understand me so far tap three times... Over."

The Amazon waited intently, then after a short interval there came three solemn taps in the loudspeaker. The assembled company glanced at each other tensely.

"Listen again," the Amazon resumed. "You will take off your hood and test the conditions for a few moments. If you sense no trace of compulsion you can be assured it has gone forever, and can broadcast the fact to your own people and to the neighbor worlds. You will signify compulsion has gone by two taps to signify 'Yes.' If I should be wrong, which I don't think I am, you have time to restore your hood and signify 'No' by one tap… Make your test. Over to you."

There was a long pause and dead silence in the control room; then from the speaker came two distinct taps. The Amazon heaved a long sigh of relief.

"Then the trouble's done with," she said into the microphone. "I am sending Tulan to the telepathic radio in the spaceship and he can take any further message you may wish to give… It is a time of rejoicing, my friend. You are free—all of you. Over and out."

The Amazon switched off and glanced at Tulan expectantly. He gave a quick nod and pushed his way through the assembly to the airlock.

"The easiest battle we ever won," Abna said thoughtfully, staring at the dead Und. "We came all prepared for trouble: he nearly annihilated us, but something stopped him—for which heaven be praised. But what *was* that something?"

"We're going to find out," the Amazon responded. "He's not been dead so long that machines can't still read the last impressions in his brain. And in this vessel we have the best Brain-Reader ever invented."

Stooping, she hauled the dead weight of Und onto her shoulder and walked quickly with him across the control room. She finally dumped him in a chair and then busied herself with an apparatus that projected a violet-tinted ray. In silence the assembly watched a nearby screen upon which, after a moment, there appeared a scene viewed through Und's eyes. The Crusaders placed it immediately as Und's Manual, the keys with which he had a planet at his command.

Then the view began to change and the manual shifted out of sight to a higher elevation. Machines began to pass by at each side of the screen as, evidently, Und moved forward. The low wall of his 'enclosure' gave way before a door and the view still progressed forward until it halted at a wide area amidst a conglomeration of further machines.

"As I see it," the Amazon said, "Und has got out of his chair and advanced forward on the trunk of his body. Everything has moved upwards from his viewpoint due to the shortness of his body. At the present moment it looks to me as though we're viewing the space—empty at the moment—where we found the *Ultra*. Yes, I was right!" she broke off, as upon the screen there gradually appeared a hazy outline and then a concrete reality of the vast spaceship.

"Evidently brought into visibility by the operation of keys on the manual," the Amazon commented.

"It was there all the time but rendered invisible," Abna said. "I don't know why we never thought of that! And our own transference from it was obviously an applied aspect of the fourth dimension..."

He broke off as the view started moving forward again. The screen mirrored the side of the *Ultra*, growing ever larger, and concentrating solely on the airlock. Then from the bottom edge of the screen two huge hands reached out—as seen through Und's eyes—and snapped back the external clamps of the airlock.

The operculum swung wide and the view proceeded through the air-conditioning chamber, into the control room, and across to the Thought Amplifier.

The view elevated abruptly as Und evidently seated himself before the Amplifier. The Amplifier slowly enlarged itself to a vision of its control panel, Und's grotesquely enlarged hand reaching out towards it. Then suddenly—

Chaos!

Stars and whirling festoons of light cascaded across the screen. The color selector showed a riot of mad hues, interwoven with an insane patchwork of dots, flashes, and huge explosions. Even though Und was dead there was still enough life left in his brain to give these pictures—and with the pictures there was emanated a curious, distracting aura of terror and screaming madness. The assembly could sense it in that pictured riot of a brain gone berserk. When it blanked abruptly into darkness it left them shaken and curiously afraid.

At last the Amazon reached out and switched the instrument off. She looked at the drawn faces of Abna, Viona, and Mexone: she sensed the disturbed, scared thoughts of Tulan, Juggernaut, and the rest of the assembly.

"If you still don't understand what happened, I'll enlighten you," she said quietly. "Maybe I sensed it more clearly because at one period I unexpectedly glimpsed the future for a moment, and I told Und as much. His vast scheme for the control of six worlds of his own creating ended in his complete insanity— an insanity of such appalling proportions that it killed him at the very moment he was planning total destruction. You sensed that insanity conveyed through the pictures from his not-quite-dead brain...

"As to why he became insane...it was what you might call a telepathic boomerang, which destroyed him. We know he was concentrating all his mental power into the machines for controlling the people of the six planets: we know those thoughts were full of murder and hatred. But what happened? Eighty percent of the populations involved were protected by hoods, which deflected the thoughts back into the projection stream down which they were traveling from the source. As a rubber ball bounces back to the thrower when it hits a wall; as the sun reflects its blinding light when you accidentally look into a mirror that is turned towards it—so Und got the reflection of his own vicious, highly amplified thoughts from the tens of thousands of hoods reflecting them. He had time to get as far as the Amplifier when, presumably, he had gathered from instruments that his maximum compulsion effort had failed—then, at the moment he was reaching out to the Amplifier switches the re-bounded thoughts struck him, destroying his brain with their amplified violence..."

"So passes Und," came the thoughts of Juggernaut.

"If he had never attempted to amplify his thoughts to such a degree he would never have suffered so violently from the rebound."

"Exactly," Abna agreed. "And but for our suggesting hoods he would never have needed to amplify his compulsion anyway. So it all fits in—"

He paused as Tulan suddenly reappeared in the control room. His thoughts were reflecting the high spirits and gratitude he obviously felt.

"I communicated," he 'thought' as the Amazon glanced at him inquiringly. "There is no doubt that all compulsion has ceased, on every one of our planets. For the first time since we were created we are free to go our own way. Apparently, as near as can be estimated, compulsion ceased about the time we landed on this planet."

"Which must have been about the time when Und decided to use the Zero-Amplifier," the Amazon mused. "Yes, as you said, Abna, it all fits in."

"There is no doubt that Und is dead?" Tulan asked anxiously; then he glanced towards him huddled in the nearby chair. "But you have moved him. Why?"

"To ascertain what really happened," the Amazon answered. "A very grim story it is, too. Since you were not here when we investigated his dead brain I'll give you the facts."

Tulan listened in silence as she related the details. At the conclusion his face was expressionless as usual but his thoughts were grim.

"How much more sensible he would have been,

Amazon, had he cast in his lot with you—then all of you could have used your scientific power to good advantage. As it is he met his death and you have gained but little for your struggle."

"You call your freedom a little thing?" the Amazon smiled.

"That is our benefit—not yours. What have you got personally?"

"A great deal of satisfaction, as we always do when we free a person or a race from a needless tyranny. We know that you now have everything you need. Your freedom, this scientific planet to use as you wish, and liberty throughout the eternal centuries to come."

"We can never be grateful enough," Tulan said.

"That we all of us know from the quality of your thoughts..." The Amazon glanced at Juggernaut. "And you, my friends, imprisoned in that unwieldy body. You have the chance now, with the scientific powers around you on this planet, to separate your four brains and create new bodies in which to house them."

"That will surely be done—in time," Juggernaut responded. "We do not regret what we did. It produced freedom in the end... And you, my friends, what are you going to do now? Stay with us?"

"No." The Amazon shrugged. "Our task here is completed. We shall travel further and see what else turns up—but we shall think of you often."

She turned and looked at the assembly, then back at Und in the chair. Cold contempt came to her exquisite features.

"Take this out with you," she said briefly. "Bury it. Burn it. But destroy it. And let us hope he was really the last of the Valdonians!"

* * * *

Six hours later the *Ultra* was well away from the planet of Und and the nearby system of six planets. Twelve hours and it had vanished into infinity as though it had never been. Also vanished, even as Abna had foreseen, was their natural telepathic ability, as their brains adjusted to their human bodies and bloodstream. Only Abna retained his original abilities, born of his metaphysical training.

The four Crusaders, the *Ultra* under automatic control, sat in the broad well of the observation window gazing out onto the coldly winking stars of the Milky Way.

"And now what?" Viona asked. It was somehow comforting to hear her own voice again. "A respite in space? A kind of cosmic holiday—?"

"Holidays never did anybody any real good," the ever-active Amazon answered briefly. "The end of one experience is but the beginning of another."

"Another?" Abna asked, as she gazed into space. "Why, what have you on mind?"

"I'm interested in that," she responded nodding her blonde head—and the others gazed with her in silent puzzlement and interest.

Ahead of the *Ultra*, at an indeterminate distance, loomed a curiously triangular formation, traced out by three points of varicolored light. They had come into being with completely suddenness against the utter blackness of empty space.

For a long time the four looked at the strange formation, then Viona's eyes became mystified.

"What are they, anyway?" she asked. "They can't be planets, surely?"

"Not with Und dead," Mexone commented dryly.

"For such mysteries as this we travel the void," the Amazon smiled, then without another word she got up and crossed to the control board.

Under the manipulation of the switches the vast nose of the *Ultra* slowly swung round in the deeps until it was pointed directly at the shining enigma in the depths.

Swiftly, unnoticeably, velocity increased.

ABOUT THE AUTHOR

British writer **JOHN RUSSELL FEARN** was born near Manchester, England, in 1908. As a child he devoured the science fiction of Wells and Verne, and was a voracious reader of the Boys' Story Papers. He was also fascinated by the cinema, and first broke into print in 1931 with a series of articles in *Film Weekly*.

He then quickly sold his first novel, *The Intelligence Gigantic*, to the American magazine, *Amazing Stories*. Over the next fifteen years, writing under several pseudonyms, Fearn became one of the most prolific contributors to all of the leading US science fiction pulps, including such legendary publications as *Astounding Stories*, *Startling Stories*, *Thrilling Wonder Stories*, and *Weird Tales*.

During the late 1940s he diversified into writing novels for the UK market, and also created his famous superwoman character, The Golden Amazon, for the prestigious Canadian magazine, the Toronto *Star Weekly*. In the early 1950s in the UK, his fifty-two novels as "Vargo Statten" were bestsellers, most notably his novelization of the film, *Creature from the Black Lagoon*.

Apart from science fiction, he had equal success with westerns, romances, and detective fiction, writing an amazing total of 180 novels—most of them in a period of just ten years—before his early death in 1960. His work has been translated into nine languages, and continues to be reprinted and read worldwide.

MORE BORGO PRESS TITLES BY
JOHN RUSSELL FEARN

THE ANJANI SERIES

The Gold of Akada: A Jungle Adventure Novel
Anjani the Mighty: A Lost Race Novel

THE BLACK MARIA SERIES

Black Maria, M.A.: A Classic Crime Novel
The Murdered Schoolgirl: A Classic Crime Novel
One Remained Seated: A Classic Crime Novel
Thy Arm Alone: A Classic Crime Novel
Death in Silhouette: A Classic Crime Novel

THE HERBERT THE DINOSAUR SERIES

A Thing of the Past
The Genial Dinosaur

OTHER BOOKS

1,000-Year Voyage: A Science Fiction Novel
Account Settled: A Science Fiction Mystery
Bury the Hatchet: A Crime Tale
A Case for Brutus Lloyd: A Science Fiction Mystery
The Crimson Rambler: A Crime Novel
Don't Touch Me: A Crime Novel
Dynasty of the Small: Classic Science Fiction Stories
The Empty Coffins: A Mystery of Horror
The Fourth Door: A Mystery Novel
From Afar: A Science Fiction Mystery
Fugitive of Time: A Classic Science Fiction Novel
The G-Bomb: A Science Fiction Novel
Here and Now: A Science Fiction Novel
Into the Unknown: A Science Fiction Tale
Last Conflict: Classic Science Fiction Stories

Legacy from Sirius: A Classic Science Fiction Novel
The Man from Hell: Classic Science Fiction Stories
The Man Who Was Not: A Crime Novel
Manton's World: A Classic Science Fiction Novel
Moon Magic: A Novel of Romance (as Elizabeth Rutland)
One Way Out: A Crime Novel (with Philip Harbottle)
Pattern of Murder: A Classic Crime Novel
Reflected Glory: A Dr. Castle Classic Crime Novel
Robbery Without Violence: Two Science Fiction Crime Stories
Rule of the Brains: Classic Science Fiction Stories
Shattering Glass: A Crime Novel
The Silvered Cage: A Scientific Murder Mystery
Slaves of Ijax: A Science Fiction Novel
Something from Mercury: Classic Science Fiction Stories
The Space Warp: A Science Fiction Novel
The Time Trap: A Science Fiction Novel
Valley of Pretenders: Classic Science Fiction Stories
Vision Sinister: A Scientific Detective Thriller
Voice of the Conqueror: A Classic Science Fiction Novel
What Happened to Hammond? A Scientific Mystery
Within That Room!: A Classic Crime Novel
World Without Chance: Classic Science Fiction Stories